TAKE LIVES

RADA JONES MD

APOLODOR

APOLODOR PUBLISHING

TAKE LIVES

1

A LUCRATIVE DEAL

In Istanbul's sweltering heart, sleazy deals are made in the shadows and trust is thinner than cigarette smoke, I think, and I stuff my cigarette into the full ashtray, observing the man perched up in the *Sea Horse's* crane. He doesn't look happy, but then he never does. For three days now, I've watched him operate the machine with his mouth pursed like he's sucking on a lemon as they provision the ship.

Whether plastic-wrapped packs of toilet paper as big as a sedan, heavy wooden crates of canned tomatoes, or massive bags bulging with watermelons, everything gets lifted from the pier in yellow nets, then stacked on the deck for the fork-lifts to load into the ship's bowels. It takes the half a dozen men hours to do it. The forklift operators sometimes switch, but the sour man on the crane is always there, telling everyone else what to do. That's why I chose him.

When they're done, I wait for him to get off, then stop by his side and offer him a cigarette. An old scar mars his right cheek, pulling his lip into a snarl as he measures me with narrowed eyes.

"You can't smoke here," he says.

"Where, then?" I ask. "I have an offer for you."

He glances at the fake Rolex I bought for ten bucks in Alexandria, and at my shiny Bontoni shoes before looking into my eyes.

"What offer?"

"A business offer. I'll pay you well for a few minutes of your time."

He glances at the other workers. They're still fussing on the deck with the provisions, so he nods for me to follow him. A low metal door takes us to a cramped corridor opening into a tiny outdoor space closed on three sides. By the acrid smell of old smoke and the sand bucket full of cigarette butts, this must be the crew's smoking space, but there's nobody here right now. I offer him a fag. He takes it, smells it, then lights it cautiously.

"What's your name?" I ask.

"Jacopo," he says. "Who wants to know?"

"Call me Artsy."

"What do you have for me, Artsy?"

"I have a package I need to move."

"From where to where?"

"From here to Dubai."

"How big?"

"Six feet by three by four."

"How heavy?"

"Two hundred pounds or so."

"What's in it?"

"My high school souvenirs."

He smiles. His two front teeth are missing, and the other ones are stained, making me wish he were frowning instead.

"Like what?"

"You don't need to know. As a matter of fact, you don't

want to know. The less you know, the happier you'll be. All you need to know is that it will make you good money."

"How much?"

"A thousand dollars now. Another one when I get it back."

He laughs, then snorts, coughs, and chokes, making my stomach twist.

"You need to stop smoking," I say.

"You need to stop making bad jokes. If you think I'll take a crate like that for two thousand dollars, you must be crazy."

"How much?"

"Depends on what's inside. Is it a stowaway?"

My jaw drops. The thought never crossed my mind. Why would you stow away from Turkey to Dubai when you can just buy a plane ticket? But then I remember that dude, the Nissan executive who escaped Japan in a cello case. I guess that could happen.

"No stowaway."

"Is it a body?"

"No body either."

"Drugs then? Do you have any idea what they'd do to me in Dubai if they caught me with a crate of cocaine? Or whatever?"

"No. Not drugs. There's absolutely nothing to worry about."

"Sure there is. If there wasn't, you'd just bring it aboard in a suitcase. What is it? Gold?"

"No gold either." I look around, making sure nobody can hear us.

"It's art."

"Art?"

"Yes. I'm an art dealer, and I was commissioned to purchase an antique Greek statue for a Dubai collector. It's a life-size marble statue of Diana. Nothing else. No drugs, no gold, no bodies."

"Why hide it, then?"

"It so happens that the person who sold it to me doesn't have papers to prove its ownership, so I can't bring it through customs. That's why I need a more discreet way to ship it."

His sooty eyes weigh on me like he's trying to read the truth inside. I smile and offer him another cigarette.

"What do you say? There's nothing dangerous — no drugs, no gold, no stowaway. It's something of no value to anyone else but me."

"And the actual owner."

"That one's long gone. Nobody even knows who that was."

He looks at me and his narrow little eyes glow with greed.

"I'll do it for a hundred thousand. Up front."

"What a comedian you are," I say, lighting another cigarette. "I like a sense of humor in a man, but I'm not here to trade jokes. I'm here to do business. I'll give you fifty thousand — half the day we leave, the other half when I get it back."

He chews on his scarred lip, thinking.

"Seventy, up front," he says.

I drop the cigarette and squash it with my shoe.

"It's been nice meeting you, Jacopo. It looks like you're more into jokes than into business, but that's no problem. I'll find another ship. It shouldn't be hard — there's a dozen heading that way every day."

I nod and turn to the door. He waits until I open it.

"Seventy. Half ahead, half at the end," he says.

"Deal," I say. "I'll bring it tomorrow. What time?"

"Noon. I'll send the boys to lunch. They don't need to see it. The fewer curious eyes, the better."

And the more money for you, I think, but I don't say it. I nod and head out. He asked for more than I planned, but I can get the first thirty-five by tomorrow. And he won't need the second half.

"Don't be late."

"No worries."

2

GUINNESS

I t's almost noon when Dr. Emma Steele, the passenger physician on the *Sea Horse*, Aurora Company's newest cruise ship, rings the doorbell to her friend Hanna's cabin. No one answers, and Emma worries something bad has happened. That would be nothing new. Bad things happen around Emma all the time, so much so that even Captain Van Huis suggested she should leave her black cloud at home. But Emma's black cloud won't stay home. It sticks to her wherever she goes.

A few months ago, after dealing with a string of gruesome deaths at her little rural hospital in upstate New York, Emma left her job as an ER doc and took to the seas, looking for freedom. She left her family, her home, and even her Germen shepherd Guinness, who is her best friend. Unlike her ex-husband Victor, who left her for a younger woman, and her moody daughter who only remembers her mom when she gets into trouble, Guinness feels Emma's heart and smells her thoughts just like she reads her pee-mail every morning.

But life at sea didn't bring her freedom. After only three days off in Istanbul, she's back to her job, ready to burden herself with her ship phone and her pager, the two despicable objects they have her shackled to 24/7.

She's about to ring the bell again when Hanna, her pale cheeks flushed with excitement, opens the door.

"Emma! You're back! And you brought her! Fantastic! Come in!"

Emma steps in. Guinness follows. Without waiting for a formal introduction, she sticks her long black nose into Hanna's crotch and sniffs her with enthusiastic vigor. Hanna laughs.

"Nobody's done that in a while."

She pets Guinness's dark head and scratches her behind the ears, in that hard-to-reach spot that feels so good that the dog leans into her.

After determining beyond reasonable doubt that Hanna is female, and thus Guinness's favorite gender, the dog goes on a comprehensive search mission, inspecting every nook and cranny of the cabin like she wants to buy it. She squeezes under the bed to check the suitcases, then inspects the coffee table. She doesn't touch the coffee but inhales every crumble of the chocolate croissant before heading to the bathroom to gulp some water from the porcelain bowl. Moments later, she's back. She licks her lips and wags her tail in thanks, then leaps on the bed and curls next to Hanna, laying her heavy head in her lap for a scratch.

"There now," Hanna says. "She's not shy, your girl. How old is she?"

"Almost seven. I got her when she was four, and she'd already had quite a career."

"What did she do?"

"She sniffed bombs in Afghanistan. Then she retired and she worked in personal protection. That's not why I got her, but she once saved my life."

"No wonder you love her so," Hanna said, and Guinness

flopped on her back, inviting a belly rub, then closed her eyes and fell asleep.

"Looks like she'll be fine here," Hanna says.

"Thank you for doing this for me," Emma says.

"I'm not doing it for you, Emma. Not only for you. I've always loved dogs, and I've missed them terribly. But let's talk specifics. How will this work?"

"This is her assistance dog certificate, but I don't think anyone will ask for it. If they do, tell them she's your assistance dog, and they'll let her be."

"What's she supposed to assist me with?"

"Your mobility, I guess, since that's where you have trouble. But I wouldn't count on it. If she sees a cat or a squirrel, she'll chase it and drag you along, so better be careful."

"I will."

"I'll come to take her for a walk every morning and evening. The captain arranged a sanitation area for her on the promenade deck and I took her there as we came, but she wasn't interested. But she'll get used to it. After her years in Afghanistan she must be used to going in the sand."

"Perfect. Having her here will compel me to move a little more. I always lack motivation. I wonder if she'd like to swim."

"She would, but I don't think the passengers would agree."

"Then we'll have to go when the pool is closed. What does she eat?"

"I brought a bag of dog food, but she'll eat whatever you give her. And she likes beer."

"Beer?"

"Yep. She's not much into lagers, but she won't say no to a stout."

Guinness opens her eyes and glances around. But there's no beer, so she licks Hanna's hand and curls back to sleep.

"How was your family? Did you have a good time?"

"It was excellent, but three days was plenty. I'm glad they agreed to meet me ashore instead of cruising with us."

"What did you do?"

"The touristy things. We visited the Topkapi palace and the Hagia Sofia mosque, then took a ferry to Bursa. We ate and drank too much, and bought a carpet."

"A carpet? What for?"

"We couldn't escape the pesky vendors. They are relentless and will chase you anywhere, no matter what you're doing. They even came to our table and interrupted our dinner to show us their goods. Victor's wife eventually broke down and bought a Persian for their home. It's six by eight feet and weighs forty pounds. I can't imagine how they'll carry it back."

"Victor's wife? She was there too?"

"Are you kidding? She's everywhere. But, to be honest, she's more pleasant than I thought. I'd never spent time with her, other than at social obligations, but she's fun to be with. Victor too. But the best part was knowing they weren't my problem."

"I take it you don't want your Victor back?"

"God forbid." Emma knocks on the wooden table to ward off the bad luck. Guinness leaps to the door barking viciously, ready to rip the intruder to shreds.

"There now," Hanna says. "I'd better be careful about having late night visitors."

Emma sighs.

"I'm afraid so. Unless you want the entire ship to know."

EMMA'S FIRST PATIENT

E mma left Guinness with Hanna, then proceeded down to deck three, where the medical staff's cabins are hidden behind the medical office. It's not a luxurious arrangement, but it has advantages: It comes with a short commute and friendly neighbors who value their privacy just as much as Emma does, and don't expose their rashes in the hallway to snatch a free consultation.

The medical office is closed for lunch, so Emma unlocks the door with her universal key, glad she has a moment to readjust to the ship life. She's only been gone for days, but they were so full they feel like weeks. For three days, she made her own schedule without worrying about the pager, wore whatever she wanted instead of the perpetual navy scrubs, and drank wine with lunch if she felt like it. With her family, as dysfunctional as they are, she can be herself. She no longer has to maintain the obliging professional facade, no matter how outrageous the behavior or how silly the complaint.

The waiting room is just the same. The L-shaped lobby

with its marshy-green linoleum, scratched by many boots, the four pink cafeteria chairs, the old desk, and the clunky old computer that would look more at home in a museum. All between walls so white they glare in the neon light.

The ICU, the only monitored room on the ship, centers around the heavy hospital bed, empty now, and its blank monitors. The antiquated machine on the counter that looks like a dishwasher is in fact the medical laboratory, and the dozens of shelves covering the walls from floor to ceiling are crammed with every possible piece of equipment, from state-of-the art ventilators to plastic urinals. The heavy Bright Star bag sitting in the corner is loaded with equipment for any kind of emergency, but for now, everything's quiet.

The short side of the L-shaped hall leads to the narrow X-ray room crammed with canes, crutches, and splints for the joints that easily dislocate piled on boxes of casting materials they rarely use. Beyond the two quarantine rooms and the tiny kitchen that's barely big enough for a coffee maker and a college-sized fridge, the back door leads to the crew cabins. Emma's, the only one with a porthole, is in the corner. She steps inside, drops her pack on the ratty loveseat, and glances around.

Nothing has changed. Her double bed with the wrinkled navy sheets; the old desk marred by bottle stains covered with books and the many chargers; the old boxy TV looking like a microwave; the garbage basket she forgot to empty. The cell is cramped and unglamorous, but, for the first time, it feels like home.

She loved being with her family — Taylor, Victor, and especially little Hope, who's already a handful. She even had a good time with Amber and her girls, who liked Emma more than they liked their mother, so they didn't leave her for a moment. Playing tourist and chatting was fun, but also exhausting. It took lots of emotional energy to anticipate Taylor's fickle moods and avoid being alone with Victor, who gave her longing looks. Making sure the kids didn't run into traffic, eat something lethal, or drink non-potable water was a full-time job. So was holding on to Guinness, who stuck to her like a limpet until she glimpsed one of the ubiquitous haughty Turkish cats and attempted some hopeless wild chase.

But, now that she's finally alone, Emma can finally hear herself think, despite the overzealous AC's loud hum. She's trying to decide whether to take a nap or go get some lunch when her pager beeps. *There we go*, she thinks. No need to worry what to do, just keep with the program. She grabs her doctor's bag she goes nowhere without and heads out.

Linda, the Canadian nurse, is talking to a young woman. She's blonde, well-built, and tanned, with an impressive cleavage and a pair of ripped jeans that look like she's coming from war. Hiding behind her, an olive-skinned little girl with crinkled black hair and a ruffled dress clutches a pink dinosaur.

Linda smiles and hugs Emma.

"I wasn't sure you were back. I paged you just in case, but boy, am I glad to see you. You must tell me all about Istanbul."

"Of course. Who do we have here?"

"This is Ayisha. Ayisha is six, and she's been coughing and having some trouble breathing. Aren't you, Ayisha?"

The child nods but doesn't speak. Her big dark eyes swallow half of her face as she gawks at Emma with fear.

"Will you give me a shot?" she whispers.

"I hope not, but let's see what's going on. I'm Dr. Steele," she tells the woman.

"Glad to meet you. I am Christine. Christine Burns. This is my daughter Ayisha."

"Good to meet you both," Emma says, and takes them to her office where she helps Ayisha to the examination table.

"What a pretty pink dress! Can Mommy help you take it off for a moment so I can listen to your heart and lungs?"

As mom helps her out of her dress, Ayisha's eyes stay glued to Emma. *She's still worried about that shot*, Emma thinks, as she grabs her stethoscope and gets closer.

The child's breathing is fast and shallow, and the skin between her ribs retracts with every breath. *This is asthma*, Emma thinks as she listens to her lungs. She's reassured by the whistling noise of her exhalation, which tells her that the child struggles a little, but she's still moving good air. *You only need to worry when the lungs go quiet*, Emma thinks, and sets down her stethoscope.

"Does Ayisha have a history of asthma?"

"No. Just reactive airway disease."

Emma nods. Many doctors don't like labeling a young child with asthma, since they don't want to frighten the parents, and most children grow out of it anyhow. That's why they call it reactive airway disease unless it gets so bad they can no longer avoid the diagnosis.

"Does Ayisha take any medications?"

"Albuterol as needed. Prednisone when she has a crisis. But she ran out of her albuterol last week, and between packing and everything else, I didn't get around to getting her another inhaler."

That's funny. If my child had asthma, that would be the first thing I'd pack, Emma thinks. She heads to the glass cabinets lining her office that contain every medication they have on the ship and gets an albuterol inhaler.

"You look like a big girl. You know how to use it?"

The child nods. Without hesitation, she takes two puffs.

"Well done, you! Now, let's get you some dexamethasone," Emma says, picking a vial from a shelf.

The child sobs. Her mother frowns.

"Is that really necessary? She's been much worse than this, and her doctor gave her some pills and got her better. Can't we skip the injection?"

"I'm afraid she needs the medicine, but it won't be an injection."

Ayisha sobs again.

"Seriously. Watch this," Emma says.

She checks the chart for the child's weight, then pulls the correct dose and drops it into a medication cup. She adds enough cough syrup to mask the medicine's foul taste and hands it to the child.

"Can you drink this?"

Ayisha tastes it and grimaces.

"It tastes awful, but it's still better than a shot, isn't it? What a brave girl you are. Where are you guys from?"

"London."

"What a wonderful city! And where are you going?"

"We're going to Dubai to meet her father," the mother says.

"Wow! That's an amazing trip," Emma says, wondering how this young child will handle such a long trip.

"You live in Dubai?"

The mother shakes her head.

"No. He's there for work. We're just visiting."

That's odd, Emma thinks. *They live in London, and they flew to Istanbul to embark on a cruise ship to sail to the father who works in Dubai. There must be plenty of direct flights from London to Dubai that would take a few hours instead of an entire month on the ship. But who knows? Maybe they have time to kill.* She counts Ayisha's breathing rate. Much better.

"How do you feel?"

"Good."

"Excellent. Why don't you take the albuterol inhaler with you and use it every four hours if you need it. And I'd like you guys to come back tomorrow morning for a recheck. Don't hesitate to call us before, if you have any trouble."

4

ARTSY

It's almost half an hour past noon, and we're still waiting in the car. My buddy Oscar parked his beat-up truck in the shade, a hundred feet from where the *Sea Horse's* crew have picked up the last provisions for this cruise. Istanbul is the last big port before Port Said, and the food is plentiful, fresh, and cheap. They can find anything in Alexandria, Haifa, or Abu Dhabi, of course, but it will cost more. That's why they've been loading tons of oranges, bananas, and melons; sacks of flour; and more crates of wine than I bothered to count.

But they stopped at noon. Since then, there's been no one there but Jacopo, chain smoking where he's not supposed to be. Now he stares down the road like he's waiting for something, and I know exactly what. He's waiting for me.

My timing is tight, but I needed to wait and make sure he hasn't summoned some welcoming committee to surprise me. But it doesn't look like it. He may not believe what I told him, but he wants the money. Badly. He just needs a plausible story to tell if they catch him. One that won't land him in jail, or even worse, on death row, or wherever they keep them in Dubai before stoning them to death.

But nothing seems amiss, so I tell Oscar to get moving. The old engine coughs and sputters before rolling us toward the *Sea Horse*.

Jacopo stares intently, but he can't see a thing through the tinted windows. I step out and shake his hand.

"Good to see you, my friend."

His ugly scar tightens into a snarl, and he glares at me like I spoke ill of his mother.

"Where the heck have you been? I said noon!"

"I know. But better late than never, isn't it? I'm here now. Should we proceed?"

He huffs with frustration and looks inside the truck. He frowns at my refrigerated container. It's bright white and brand new and not much bigger than a coffin.

"Refrigerated? Why?"

"So I can lock it and make sure nobody tries to peek inside."

"I don't know about that. That thing must be heavier than a son of a gun. And where the heck do I put it?"

"You'll figure it out. For thirty-five thousand, it's worth it."

"Seventy, I said. Thirty-five now, the other thirty-five when you get it back."

"Of course. That's what I meant," I say, cursing my stupid mouth. "But not now. Tonight, when you show it to me. I need to make sure it really ended up on the ship, not somewhere on the bottom of the sea."

"You don't trust me, do you?"

I laugh. "I didn't get this old by trusting people. And neither did you. There's the money."

I open my sports coat to let him peek at the money vest underneath. Truth be told, it's just a fishing vest with oodles of pockets, but there's a pile of new 100-dollar bills in each of them. A sight to behold. Smoother than a package and harder to steal.

His eyes count the pockets, but I button my sports coat before he gets to count the notes. He's got lasers in his eyes, this dude.

"I want to see the statue."

"You must be kidding. You want me to open it here? I thought you were in a hurry."

"The less we talk, the faster it goes. I won't get this on the ship before I see what's inside it," he says, and he means it. Something spooked him out.

"Are you sure? Don't you think the less you know, the better off you'll be?"

He shakes his head.

"I see it now or the deal is off."

Like really? What's wrong with people these days? There's no more trust.

I glance at Oscar, who sits at the wheel playing with his phone like none of this is his business.

"OK."

I press the code to unlock the box with Jacopo watching. It's a simple four-digit code, so he'll have no trouble opening the box when I'm not watching. But I'm OK with that. I'd rather he unlock it than break it open.

The lock clicks. I pull the lid open to the bubble wrap inside.

I pull out my Swiss knife and cut the bubble wrap just enough to show him a white arm ending in a hand with broken fingers.

"Good enough?"

Jacopo nods and heads to his crane. Ten minutes later, the box is on the deck, waiting for the forklift to take it, and Jacopo is back. I offer him a cigarette.

"What time and when?" I ask.

"The safety drill is at four. That's a good time, since everyone's busy. But won't you need to be at the drill?"

"I'll figure it out. Where do I find you?"

"Meet me in front of the medical office. If anyone asks what you need, tell them you have a headache and you need some aspirin. But don't be late again!"

"I won't."

5

LUNCH

"Lunch?" Linda asks, after locking the medicals office door behind Ayisha and her mom.

"Sure. Crew mess?"

"Where else?" Linda points at her scrubs. "There's no time to change into civilian clothes to go eat upstairs. No point either. The last thing I want to do is get between the new passengers and their food."

Emma laughs, but Linda is right. The first day of every cruise, the lunch buffet testifies to the survival of the fittest. The countless temptations of the all-you-can-eat buffet are hard to resist, and the new guests have a hard time choosing, so they grab it all. The prime rib and the roasted chicken and the baked salmon and the salads and the fifteen mouth-watering desserts, all looking better than they taste. But they won't know until they try, so try them, they do, with abandon. It's wise to get out of their way.

Emma and Linda head to the crew mess, a few doors down on deck three, which is the place where crew life happens. The shore excursion office is down the hall, and the crew bar is right next to Human Resources, a handy place to grab a drink after getting dressed down for some entitled passenger's complaint. The many invisible cogs essential to the workings of the ship are all down here, hidden from the passengers' eyes, since, with the notable exception of the medical office, deck three is reserved for the crew. That's where they buy internet cards from the dispensing machines; learn about crew parties, soccer meets, and crew excursions from the posters pinned on a corkboard; or buy and sell cameras, iPhones, and sunglasses.

This afternoon the crew mess is almost empty. The ship departs in a couple of hours, so the crew is too busy to linger over lunch. The stewards rush to prepare the new passengers' cabins, setting them up with fresh fruit and towels folded like squirrels; the cooks chop tons of onions and sweat over tonight's welcome dinner, while the sailors ready the ship for departure. The entertainers and the spa staff loiter along the staircase and the hallways to help the newcomers find their way. Only the medical staff is not yet on the hook, but that may change in a blink.

Dana, the Romanian nurse, sits at a table in the corner with a man, picking at some green shredded salad. Her face lights up as she sees them, and she waves them over.

"We're coming," Linda says, grabbing a tray to check the day's specials.

Unlike the Sea View Buffet with its lavish displays, the crew mess is a cafeteria. You get in line and pick your main dish, which is Asian, then put together a salad, and grab dessert. Sometimes there's pizza or pasta, but Western food is rare since the crew is half Indonesian and half Philippine, so the company makes a point of cooking their comfort foods to help them feel closer to home.

Emma struggled at first, but she no longer breaks in a cold sweat when bulging fish eyes stare at her from the broth, or unidentified things wiggle away from the serving tongs. She tells herself it must be pasta or mushrooms, since they wouldn't cook worms on the ship, and moves on. There's nothing a little Tabasco can't fix. And, if everything fails, there's always ice cream.

Today's offerings are new to her. The first one is a creamy orange liquid with brown rag-like shreds floating between red chili peppers and green onions. The second is murky brown, with round eggplant slices and whole green chilies swimming between white fish heads and translucent strings of curly pork skin.

Emma sighs. She helps herself to some of the orange stuff, then follows Linda to Dana's table. Her friend hugs her and introduces her to the man.

"This is Doctor Basuki Saleh, our new crew doctor. He's from Bali."

The new crew doctor is a handsome brown man with a thin mustache and a carefully tended short beard. Shiny strands of black hair fall over his dark eyes with lashes so long they look fake.

He greets Emma with a dazzling smile and stands to pull her chair. It's been so long since that happened that Emma does a double take to make sure he's pulling it for her.

"Thank you, Doctor. You are from Bali? What a wonderful place. We stopped there recently, and I found it fascinating. Bali must be the most amazing place in Indonesia," Emma says.

"We think so," the doctor says. "We like to consider ourselves a cut above the rest of Indonesia. Call me Basuki, please. May I call you Emma?"

"Of course. How do you like the *Sea Horse*?"

"So far, so good. It's newer and better equipped than the *Sea Star*, where I had my last contract. And I could hardly hope for a more charming team."

His eyes shift from Emma to Dana, then Linda, and back,

and Emma's heart sinks. She hopes he's not like Fajar, her first crew doctor, who couldn't resist bedding every woman he met. But at least he wasn't a grumpy drug addict, like Dr. Majok. Or a psychopath, like Mariko. In only a few months, Emma had had her share of rather peculiar colleagues, and would prefer not to add Basuki to that list.

"I guess you haven't yet met Sue," she says, and they all choke with laughter.

The steam wafting up from her bowl fills her nose with aromas of lemongrass and garlic, making her mouth water. She stirs it, and some brown muddy rags float to the top. She tries to identify them but she can't, so she wonders whether to move on to ice cream.

"You got the soto betawi? How do you like it?" Basuki asks.

"I don't know yet. What is it?"

"It's a traditional Javanese soup. Beef simmered with lemongrass, bay leaves, galangal, garlic, and shallots. The coconut milk makes it creamy, and the fried shallots add a bit of a crunch. I love it."

Relieved that it's beef instead of something more exotic, Emma tastes it. It's delicious, spicy and bursting with flavor, and she eats it with gusto, glad she gave the fish heads a miss. But, as it often happens, she's only half done when her pager goes off. She curses under her breath and heads back to Medical, leaving her soto betawi behind.

6

HEADACHE

The medical office is empty but for Sue, the lead nurse, who sits at the desk scrolling through Facebook, and Emma's mouth fills with bile. *This is just another one of Sue's petty harassments,* she thinks.

There have been plenty, since Sue hated Emma from the day they met. Whether it was because she didn't like taking orders — and a doctor's job is to give orders to nurses — or because she didn't like seeing Will, her husband, being friendly to Emma, or maybe just because she's the kind of person who enjoys pulling the wings out of flies, Sue made it her mission to torture Emma. She woke her from sleep to remind her of some silly assignment that wasn't due for weeks, interrupted her lunch to ask her some asinine question, and took every opportunity to annoy her. And God knows there were plenty. Still, after working together for months, they seemed to have reached some sort of truce, and they ignored each other when possible. But that seems to be a thing of the past.

"What can I do for you?" Emma asks.

"There's a patient in the ICU. He requested to see you."

"Me?"

"He asked for the doctor. That would be you."

"Did you suggest he should come to the clinic at five?"

"I did. But he said it was an emergency."

"What's his emergency?"

"A terrible headache, he says."

Emma sighs. That's legit. Some headaches are genuine emergencies — intracranial bleeds, blood clots, or meningitis. Most are not, but figuring out which is which is hard. She can't fault Sue for paging her, even though her smirk tells Emma how much she enjoyed interrupting her lunch. So she sighs, takes the chart, and walks into the ICU.

The room is cool, dark, and quiet. The patient lies in bed with his eyes closed, appearing asleep. He's pale and seriously overdressed in a white shirt, dark pants with lines so sharp they could draw blood, and shiny Italian shoes.

Emma checks his vitals. No fever, but his blood pressure and his pulse seem high.

"Mr. Leach?"

He nods without opening his eyes.

"I am Dr. Steele. How can I help you?"

"I need oxycodone."

Whoa, baby. Emma's heart picks up the pace. She's heard that chief complaint, or some version of it, a thousand times. Whether they need Dilaudid, Percocet, or fentanyl, the afflicted individuals are usually in too much pain to open their eyes, and they can't be bothered to answer questions or cooperate with the exam.

Nine times out of ten, the problem turns out to be a drug dependency, and when Emma refuses their fix, they get angry and abusive. Sometimes just verbally, calling her words unfit to print as they dash to the door, but others get physically aggressive. Emma had her car keyed and her tires cut, but she had it easy. Some of her colleagues, nurses and doctors, got threatened and physically hurt, and, worst of all, her beloved mentor got slaughtered in his car by an addict. Emma does her best to feel sympathy and show compassion, but it's easier said than done. She sighs and steps back, but keeps her voice soft and her manner professional.

"That is interesting. What makes you think you need oxycodone?"

"I have a splitting migraine, and nothing else helps."

"You have a history of migraines?"

"Yes."

"Is this headache typical of your migraines?"

"Yes."

"When did it start?"

"This morning."

"What were you doing when it started?"

"Sleeping."

"Did it reach maximal intensity immediately, or did it get worse over time?"

"It got worse."

"Would you please describe your headache for me?"

The man jumps to his feet like a scalded cat. His dark eyes shaded by bushy eyebrows knitted in a frown glare at Emma as he juts out his clefted chin and growls.

"Listen, Doctor, I'm not here to keep you entertained. I am in severe pain and I need help. Will you help me or not?"

"I'll be glad to help you as soon as I determine the best way to do it. Once I determine you have a migraine, as opposed to something that might kill you, I'll be glad to give you the appropriate treatment for migraines. Which, by the way, is not oxycodone."

"I know my body. That's the only thing that works for me."

Oh, boy. How many times have I heard this one? Emma wonders.

"I understand. However, oxycodone is not a good treatment for migraines. Multiple studies have determined beyond a shadow of a doubt that opioids do not help migraines. They make them worse."

"Listen, Doctor, I'll take the risk. Now, will you give me what I need or not?"

"I'll be glad to give you the recommended migraine treatment."

"Which is?"

"Either a triptan, or a combination of an NSAID and an antiemetic. With an antihistamine to ensure that you won't suffer any untoward effects."

"That won't help me."

"I regret I can't give you something that will not help you and might be detrimental to your health. I am sorry."

"You should be. Do you know who I am?"

Emma glances at the chart.

"Mr. Leach, I believe?"

He turns purple and glowers at her with such fury that Emma steps back, worried he'll punch her. But he only bites his lip and sticks his fists in his well-pressed trousers.

"I plan to see the captain about this, you know."

Emma sighs. She'd rather walk in high heels and naked into tonight's cocktail party than have Captain Van Huis lecture her again. But she has no choice. She's had plenty of unpleasant conversations with the captain. What's one more between friends?

"I'm sure he can't wait to hear from you."

His face twisted with rage, the man turns around and leaves. His heavy steps fade down the hallway, and Emma draws in a deep breath. This cruise hasn't even started, and she's already in trouble, but there was nothing else she could do. She couldn't give him opioids just because he asked for them. That's what started the damn opioid crisis, and there's no sign it will ever stop.

She sits in the chair by the door and closes her eyes, counting her breaths to slow down her heart. 1-2-3 in, 1-2-3 hold, 1-2-3 out, then repeat.

"Emma?"

Sue stands in the door, her eyes narrowed. *She must be loving this,* Emma thinks.

"Well done."

JACOPO'S PAY

Jacopo is late.

The general alarm wails throughout the ship, and hundreds of harried feet climb up and down the stairs looking for the muster stations. The mandatory safety drill has started. All passengers must attend, but the elevators are out, and I wonder how they'll cart those who can't climb stairs. It would be good to know.

I stand by the medical office's closed door, and that gives me an idea. I should check out this place; they might have something I could use. But not now. Now, I need to find out where my stuff is and pay Jacopo. Where the heck is he?

Just as I'm losing my patience, he appears through a heavy metal door marked "Crew only" and signals me to follow. One after the other, we stride down an empty gray hallway edged with doors on both sides. I check them out so I can find my way back as I follow him down the stairs to the deck below. It's empty and quiet down here. The alarm has finally stopped, and there's no sound other than our feet pounding the metal deck.

"In here," Jacopo says.

We turn left into a space as big as a hangar, crammed with tall, heavy shelves loaded with boxes, cases, buckets, ropes, pipes, and whatever else they might need to fix whatever goes wrong on the ship. There are oodles of stuff piled everywhere, in no apparent order, but Jacopo seems to know exactly what's what, and he points to my box in the corner. It's hard to see it under all the boxes piled on top of it, but it's there, all right, so I nod.

"Good job. How do I find you to recover it?"

"Just like you found me to get it here. My money?"

"Of course."

I take off my coat, then the loaded fishing vest and hand it to him. His face lights up like a Christmas tree as he unzips his mechanic's jumper to put on the vest underneath.

As he struggles to get his arms out of his sleeves, I pull on my gloves and grab the vial out of my pocket. He's still undoing buttons as I grab him by the throat. I hold my breath as I stick the cannula up his nostril and squeeze, squirting it all in. Before I count to five, he goes slack and I let him fall to the ground.

Still holding my breath, I lob the vial and the gloves as far as I can in the room, grab the vest, and rush to the door. Once I'm in the hallway, I stop to take a deep breath, then put on my money vest and button my coat over it. Well done.

I hustle back the way I came, trying to look casual, but I know I'm in big trouble if anyone sees me. On the second deck I'm too far in the ship's belly to pretend I got lost.

I climb the stairs to the upper deck, then walk by the row of labeled doors like I know what I'm doing. I'm almost at the exit to the passenger's quarters when a woman wearing a white coat steps out of the medical office, staring at the papers she's holding.

I freeze. Should I keep going or stay put, hoping she doesn't notice me? Because if she sees me, I can't let her live.

When they find Jacopo, she'll remember seeing me where I don't belong, and the last thing I need is a witness.

She turns her back to me and steps out with her nose still in those papers. I count to five, then follow her out and breathe a sigh of relief. Thank Allah!

8

THE CAPTAIN'S WELCOME PARTY

I t's past seven, and, as usual, Emma is late for the welcome cocktail party. The evening clinic ran late, since everybody and their neighbor stopped by to say hi and confirm there really was a doctor on the ship, should they need one. Some came to store their insulin in the medical refrigerator, others needed to replace the medications they forgot to bring, but most were just being social, and nobody was sick. Still, the one-hour clinic turned into two, then two and a half by the time they put everything away and prepared the equipment for any possible emergency.

Emma took fifteen minutes to shower, twist her wet hair in a low bun and slip into her old black cocktail dress. It remains her favorite, because it's so basic nobody notices she wears it to every cocktail party and formal dinner. Or at least they don't say they do. But what else can Emma do when three quarters of her luggage is taken by medical books and dog food? To dress it up a little, she puts on red lipstick and grabs the scarf Victor bought her in Istanbul. With its rich hues of blue, green, and gold, it resembles a peacock's tail and turns Emma's plain black dress into a showpiece.

This flashy scarf is like nothing else Emma owns. It screams "look at me," and that's the last thing Emma needs. That's why, when Victor tried to buy it for her, she declined, but he wouldn't take no for an answer. Not even when his current wife, Amber, glared at him with a growing irritation that would have deterred more observant men.

"Please take it. It brings out the color of your eyes," Victor said. He took Emma's hand, and she pulled it back.

"Thank you, but I don't need it. It's beautiful, but it's not my thing. Much too showy. Where would I even wear it?"

"To the glamorous dinners on the ship?"

"Can't you see she doesn't want it?" Amber said, her dry voice a tad louder than needed. Then Taylor intervened.

"Take it, Mother. You deserve to have something beautiful."

Hearing Taylor say something nice to her was so shocking that Emma accepted the gift, and now she's glad.

She wiggles her way through the sea of sweaty bodies squeezed in shiny dresses and sports coats, trying to avoid knocking people's glasses. She looks right and left for Hanna and Guinness, but they're nowhere to be seen.

Dark-clad waiters carry platter after platter of long-stemmed glasses with bubbly, fragile pastries, and delicate shrimpy canapés. To add to the cheer, the band plays hits from the '80s, reminding guests of the good old days. Only Captain Van Huis, more popular than a queen bee amid a swarm, seems immune to the cheer. His irked expression shows he'd rather be anywhere else but here, and Emma can't help but chuckle. She waves off Antonio's desperate call to free him from the dozen ladies vying for his attentions and moves on. They don't know that handsome Antonio is not into ladies.

She's about to give up and leave when a hand grasps her shoulder. Emma's heart skips a beat. Before stopping to think, she pivots, ready to throw the punch Antonio taught her, but she sees who grabbed her and her panic turns into delight.

"Nok! You are back!"

Nok, Emma's friend and Captain Van Huis's wife, looks stunning. Her red dress hugs curves that steal men's eyes, and her glowing skin turns women green with envy. But she only has eyes for Emma.

They hug; then Nok turns to the man by her side.

"Emma, let me introduce you to my friend Archie. Mr. Archibald Bennett Leach is our new lecturer, specializing in archeology. This charming lady is my friend Dr. Emma Steele, the ship's physician."

"How do you do?" the man says, in a hi-so English that would put King Charles to shame. He sports the same fancy shoes, well-pressed pants, and the same cleft in his chin that he did earlier in Medical, but his hateful glare mellows to a haughty gaze as he looks down his long nose at Emma.

"How do you do?" Emma replies, wondering how to make herself scarce. Their awkward encounter was bad enough when he was just some self-important guest she'd likely never see again, but if he's Nok's friend and one of the lecturers, he'll be hard to avoid. Things are about to get hairy.

"Archie studied at Oxford and was involved with the Petra excavations. Even better, he went to school with Lady Di's brother, didn't you, Archie?"

Archie shrugs with aristocratic nonchalance.

"Somebody had to, hadn't they?"

Emma forces a smile, looking for an excuse to leave.

"How fascinating. Now, if you'll excuse me, I have to go look for my friend Hanna."

Nok laughs.

"You won't have to go far. Hello, Hanna. You look younger than ever."

Nok is right. With her mischievous smile, sparkling blue eyes, and the cloud of white hair surrounding her face like an aura, Hanna's beauty is ageless, and her royal blue dress makes the most of it.

"Look who's talking," Hanna says, hugging her. "How did your show go?"

"That's not something I should discuss on board, since the Aurora company doesn't regard stripping as an appropriate career for a captain's wife, but I'll tell you all about it later. Let me introduce my friend to you. Mr. Archibald Bennet Leach is *Sea Horse's* new archeology lecturer. This is my friend Hanna. She lives on the *Sea Horse.*"

"How do you do? I'm Archie." The man greets Hanna with a dazzling smile.

Stunned, Hanna stares at him without a word. When she finally shakes his hand, her wide eyes are still glued to him.

"You OK, Hanna?" Emma whispers.

Hanna nods.

"I apologize for staring like that, but you remind me of my late husband. Many years ago."

"I am honored. I am sure your husband was a remarkable man."

"That he was. Especially when he wasn't drunk."

Emma can't help but laugh. Nok does too, and Archie forces a smile.

"So you're our new archeologist? That means you'll be with us for a while?"

"Until Dubai."

"Excellent. How about we blow this joint and go somewhere quiet to get to know each other better?"

Nok sighs.

"I wish I could, but I have to stick around for a bit. This is the first night of the cruise, and Pieter counts on my playing the graceful host. But you guys go have fun. I'll catch up with you tomorrow."

"Let's go then," Hanna says.

Emma squeezes a thin smile.

"Why don't you two go? I'll go take Guinness for her evening walk, and I'll grab a bite in the crew mess later."

Hanna grabs her arm.

"Oh, no. Not so fast. Guinness is fine. She's already walked three times today, and now she sleeps like a baby. You can take her out after dinner. Let's go."

"But…"

"No but. You won't let this charming gentleman suffer through an entire dinner with only an old woman for company, will you? Let's go."

9

SMALL TALK

The Ambrosia restaurant, the *Sea Horse's* finest dining venue and Hanna's favorite, is decorated like a Chicago steak house. Between the chocolate-brown walls that dampen the noise, there are more intimate shadows than glitz and glitter. The deep leather chairs hold you in a hug, the attentive waiters glide around like friendly ghosts, and the emaciated pianist with sad eyes drops soothing notes from his spidery fingers. He's so thin that Emma can't stop wondering why. *Is he sick? One of these days I'll ask him,* she tells herself, but she won't. She'd rather befriend a snarling dog than approach people, so she knows she won't get near the pianist unless he falls unconscious or gets shot.

The aroma of charred meat, good wine, and expensive perfume reaches Emma's nostrils, and her stomach grumbles. She has eaten nothing today but that orange soup, and she didn't even get to finish that because of this pompous ass who's trailing them to the table. She would have liked to disappear on the way to the restaurant, but Hanna held on to her arm, pretending she needed help. Well, she wasn't pretending, since her bad hip has her walking with a cane, but she could have held on to this Leach person instead. But she knows Emma well enough to figure she'd try to escape.

Too late now. The maitre' d, with the air of a compassionate funeral director, pulls Hanna's chair, then Emma's, and she's trapped. She can only hope for her pager to ring, but that never happens when you need it. She'll need wine to get through this dinner.

If their scuffle hadn't been a patient encounter, Emma would have told Hanna she already met Mr. Leach. He threatened her when she offered her professional opinion, so she has no more desire to dine with him or get to know him better than she has to swim ashore from wherever the *Sea Horse* happens to be at the moment. But, since she can't share information about a patient, no matter how worthless and rude, she just bites her lip and sighs as the maitre d' presents them with the oversized menus.

"Can I start you with a drink? A cocktail, maybe?"

"I'm cocktailed out. How about some wine?" Hanna asks.

"Excellent idea. May I suggest a Puligny Montrachet: Domaine Dupont-Fahn Les Grands Champs. It's a recent addition to our cellar."

"I think Emma is more into reds. And I'm cold. I wouldn't mind something to take the chill out of these old bones," Hanna says. "You know, Archie, I think the story of male dominance started with the clothes you men had us wear."

"Really? How so?"

"While you men wear jackets and vests, you had us dress in skimpy clothes, so we'd always be cold and miserable, and need a man around to keep us warm. And you had us walk in high heels and skirts so we can't run, while you wear pants and sensible shoes to get an advantage."

"How about the tie? How's that an advantage?"

"So you can rope us in if we try to escape?"

Archie laughs. "It makes perfect sense. May I apologize and offer you some wine to atone for the role of my gender in female subjugation?"

"Now you're talking. What do you propose?"

Archie points to a wine on the maitre d's thick wine list, then turns to Hanna.

"Nok said you live on the ship?"

"I do. When my husband died, my son tried to move me to a nursing home. I moved here instead, and it's the best decision I ever made. Here on the *Sea Horse*, I have food, entertainment, housekeeping, and a built-in social life. I even get excellent healthcare," Hanna says, pointing to Emma.

"But don't you miss being outside? Walking in the park? Petting a dog?"

"Not one bit. I can go outside anytime I want, which is almost never, and I get to see new places every day. As for walking, I find it seriously overrated. I'd rather ride a motor-bike. And I just got a dog today."

"A dog? You got a dog on the ship?"

"Yes. A German shepherd named Guinness. She's my new mobility assistance companion, and she's already doing her job. She's dragged me out twice since lunch, which is more than I usually go out in a week. But enough about me. Let's talk about something more interesting. Nok said you are an archeologist?"

"Nok was right, as always."

"What exactly does an archeologist do? You dig through dirt to look for stuff?"

"Pretty much. Archeologists are very much like dogs: We dig through dirt to find bones and stuff. Except that we don't bury our own bones, and we seldom eat them."

Hanna laughs and glances at Emma, who forces a smile. Fortunately, the maitre d' is back with the wine and fusses enough to get them distracted. He presents them with a dusty bottle with the pride of a first-time father showing off his newborn son.

"This bottle looks like it came out of one of your digs," Hanna says.

The maitre d' holds it up for them to admire before wiping it with a white satin napkin, raising the dust and making Emma sneeze.

"I hope you'll enjoy it." Archie glances at Emma.

This is the first time he has addressed her after the introductions, and Emma wonders if he's trying to maintain appearances in front of Hanna.

"I'm sure I will," she says.

"This is a Saint-Julien: Chateau Lagrange 2018," the maitre d' declares. With the smooth moves of a prestidigitator, he pulls out the cork and offers it to Archie. Archie shakes his head and points to the table. His mouth tight, the maitre d' sets the rejected cork on the table like he's storing a precious Faberge egg before pouring a few drops in Archie's glass.

The archeologist sniffs it, twirls it, and sniffs again before finally tasting it. He nods, and the maitre d' pours the wine and waits for the verdict.

"To new friends," Archie says.

"To new friends," Hanna answers. Emma nods and lifts her glass.

The wine is so dark it's purple. Rich aromas of cherry and black currant rise from the glass, making Emma's mouth water. She sips, and the wine sings on her tongue.

"Nice wine," Hanna says. "I think I'll forgive you for my high heels for tonight. Now, tell me about archeology."

"How about we order first? I'll have the cioppino," Emma says, worried she'll have to listen to a whole spiel she doesn't give a hoot about and then get paged before she gets to eat dinner.

10

ARCHEOLOGY

Hanna orders the lamb chops, but Archie orders the beefsteak tartare, and Emma shudders. That means they'll get fifteen minutes in the limelight while the maitre d' makes a spectacle of stirring an egg yolk, a few chopped onions, and pickles and some condiments into the ground beef. That would take Emma thirty seconds at home. Two minutes, say, if Guinness stuck her nose into things and tried to help, as usual. But then she's cooking, not putting up a show.

"So, what do archeologists do besides dig up bones?" Hanna asks.

"We study people and cultures through every means available to us."

"I thought that was anthropology."

"They study living people. We look at the past. Since our subjects are dead, we can't watch them go about their lives and ask them questions, like anthropologists do with theirs. That's why we study every kind of remains we can find from past civilizations, whether they're artifacts or features."

"What's the difference?"

"Artifacts are portable, like arrowheads, pots, coins, and jewelry. Features are immovable, like the pyramids, old city walls, or the Stonehenge monument. But no matter what we study, we aim to understand how people of a certain era lived, how they interacted, what they believed in. And how they disappeared."

"That's interesting. I thought the arrowheads, the coins, and the broken pots were the purpose."

"Not at all. They only matter for what they teach you about the people who left them. Do you know what Margaret Mead considered the most significant archeological artifact of all time?"

"The Rosetta Stone?"

"No, though that was one of the most important discoveries ever, since it allowed us to translate the hieroglyphs."

"The Dead Sea scrolls?"

"Not them either."

"I don't know. Emma, you have any idea?"

Emma shakes her head. Not only does she have no idea, she doesn't even know who this Margaret Mead is. But this Leach person doesn't need to know that. I'll Google her later, she thinks, digging into her cioppino with gusto. The steam rising from her bowl smells like fennel, shallots, and garlic and makes her mouth water. She swore she'd never order cioppino again, because she gets paged every time she orders it. But if there's ever been a good time to get paged, it's now, she thinks, hurrying to enjoy those juicy shrimps before she has to leave.

The archeologist glances at the maitre d', who takes his sweet time mixing the tartare with the attitude of a shaman performing a life-changing ritual, then turns back to Hanna.

"Margaret Mead thought that the most important archeological discovery of all times was a healed human femur that purportedly marks the beginning of the human civilization.

As our medical expert here can confirm, people don't heal from broken femurs on their own. For someone to survive such an injury while living in some prehistoric cave, other humans must have cared for them for weeks. Someone brought them food and water and protected them from predators until they could take care of themselves. That's why she thought it to be so significant."

"Fascinating. Which findings get you most excited? Weapons? Writings? Coins?"

"None of them. I have colleagues who specialize in every one of those, but I am a bio-archeologist with a special interest in osteoarcheology. To me, there's nothing more important than human bones. I'm a bone man through and through."

"Why?"

"Because they provide more valuable information than anything else, even though finding a complete skeleton is very rare. More often, you find just a handful of bones. Sometimes only one, but even that can teach you a lot. It starts with where you found it. Say you find a metacarpal — that's a tiny bone from a finger. Was it in a church, encased in gold, like a relic? In an ossuary or a tomb? Inside someone's stomach? Those are different scenarios that help you figure out what happened to the person the bone belonged to."

"I can't argue with that," Hanna says.

"Then you examine them. Is it intact? Broken? Broken and then healed? Sawed or pierced by an arrow? Partly burned? Any of those scenarios opens several hypotheses on what happened to the person. By their size and shape, you can infer the age, gender, and maybe even the occupation of the individual the bone belonged to. Nine times out of ten, wider pelvic bones tell you that you're dealing with a woman. Arthritis or osteoporosis mean you're looking at an older person. A dominant arm stronger than the other may mean you're looking at an archer. Riders often have bowed legs because of the time they spend in the saddle. The composition of the bones informs you of their diet, especially if you happen to find teeth. Out of all human remains, I find the teeth the most intriguing — other than skulls, of course."

"Why?"

"Teeth reflect what we eat, what we do, and even who we are. In children, the degree of tooth eruption lets you determine their age. Teeth tell you not only about people's diet, but their lifestyle. Tooth decay is the destruction of the enamel by acids produced by carbohydrate-feeding bacteria. That's why grain eaters tend to have worse teeth than hunter-gatherers, who eat more protein, so dental caries indicate an agriculture-based society. Females have more caries because of the toll pregnancies and lactation take on their bodies."

"It sounds like detective work. You start with a tooth or a finger bone and build up the story of a person and maybe a whole society."

"Very much so."

"Are your stories always accurate?" Emma asks, then wishes she hadn't. She doesn't need to irk this guy more than she already did.

"Not always. Some are way off the mark, and some are totally fabricated. And sometimes we get duped. Josiah Whitney, one of the greatest American geologists, received a skull from some miners who said they found it below the ground. He dubbed it the Calaveras Skull, after the place they found it, and presented it as the oldest human remains. It took almost three decades before the Smithsonian dismissed it as a hoax. Later on, it was discovered that the miners had fooled Whitney."

"I guess anyone can make mistakes," Hanna says.

"Absolutely. Especially if they play expert in a field they know little about. Whitney should have stuck to geology and let the archeologists do their job. But we all like to think we know best."

Is he apologizing for rejecting my expertise, or telling me that he's the only expert on his body? Emma wonders. But the cioppino works its magic and her pager goes off just as the ship speakers announce a Bright Star code on deck two, the signal for a medical code. Emma drops her spoon and runs without saying goodbye.

11

LEILA

L eila glances at Ayisha to make sure she's asleep. Curled in the massive king bed with the pink dinosaur she goes nowhere without, the child looks so tiny. Her long eyelashes, soft dark curls, and her rosebud pink mouth tug at Leila's heart.

She cracks open the door and glances up and down the hallway, making sure it's empty, before taking the stairs to the deck below. She heads toward the ship's stern and knocks at the second door from the last on the left.

There's no answer, and her heart quickens with worry. She knocks again, harder this time, in the special 3-1-2 pattern they agreed upon if everything was safe.

The door cracks open to the darkness inside.

"It's me."

He grabs her by the wrist and pulls her in, then slams the door behind her.

"What the heck are you doing here?"

"I… I just wanted to make sure you're OK. Didn't you hear the signal?" she whispers, rubbing her arm where his fingers dug in. *That will leave a bruise,* she thinks.

He pushes the switch by the door, flooding the cabin in harsh light. His room is just like hers, but for the windows. He got an inside cabin, which is cheaper and has no windows for curious eyes to peek in. He wanted to get one of those for her and Ayisha as well, but that's where she put her foot down. She couldn't have Ayisha stuck with no daylight for a month, especially since he doesn't want them going out and about unless absolutely necessary. So he relented and got them a cabin with a view, but he drew the line at a balcony.

"What for? Just so the kid finds a way to get in trouble when you aren't watching her? No."

"But I watch her all the time."

"You won't now. You have work to do, remember? We aren't here on vacation."

Leila sighed and agreed, so they got the smaller cabin with a sea view, and he got this one. It's not nicer, but it's a tad bigger, so Ayisha would have more room to play. *But this is not about playing,* she thinks, watching the little muscle at the corner of his jaw twitch with every heartbeat. That's what it does whenever he clenches his teeth in fury. She wishes she didn't have to make him angry, but she didn't have a choice.

"I'm sorry, Selim, but I was worried. Then I heard that signal and I needed to make sure you were alright."

"I was just fine before you came. Did anyone see you?"

"No."

"Are you sure?"

"Yes. I looked back at every step, so I'm sure nobody followed me. The hallways were empty."

He curses heartily, and her heart skips a beat.

"What?"

"The cameras. They have freaking security cameras all over this ship. They recorded you leaving your cabin, and they recorded you coming here, without the shadow of a doubt. Fucking stupid woman," he says, punching his fist in his other palm with frustration.

"I didn't think about cameras," Leila says, her shoulders tightening with the weight of her guilt.

"You didn't think. Period. So, what do you want?"

Leila stares at him, trying to recognize the man she knows, but he's so cold and so rough. Nothing like he used to be back home when he looked at her like she was the most beautiful woman in the world. He brought her flowers and chocolate, and whispered in her ear, telling her how wonderful she was, and how she had changed his life for the better. But that was so long ago, it feels like a different life.

"I want you to like me and be nice to me, and act like I'm a person and I matter. I gave up so much to be with you, and ever since we left, you've been acting like both Ayisha and I are just a terrible annoyance. We didn't ask to be here, remember? You wanted me to come, and I did, despite my better judgement, and against the advice of my friends. But now it looks like they were right. You haven't stopped berating me for something or other ever since we left home. If we're really so much of a burden, we can go back, you know? We can get off in Çanakkale, get back to Istanbul, and catch a flight home. That will leave you free of the inconvenience, and it would be safer for my child."

Selim looks at her with those long-lashed dark eyes that stole her heart years ago, and his anger seems to vanish. His gaze changes from frustrated to loving as he takes her in his arms and holds her close.

"Oh Leila, how can you say that? You know how much I love you and Ayisha. There's no one more important in my life. I can't live without you, and I don't want to. You are the moon lighting my nights and your kisses give me life. My life wouldn't be worth living without you. Don't even think about leaving me."

His lips seek hers, and he holds her close, kissing her so deeply that her knees soften. She'd fall if he didn't hold her up, murmuring sweet words she doesn't understand. But the heat of his breath warms her ear, and she feels his heart race against her chest. Her insides melt, and she pulls him to the massive king bed taking half the room.

"Oh, my lovely, I don't think that's a good idea. What if Ayisha wakes up? What if she leaves the room and starts roaming the hallways, looking for you?"

"She won't. She never does. Come. Make love to me. I'm thirsty for you," she says, dragging him toward the bed. He follows reluctantly.

She pulls off her jeans and her panties, then undoes his belt and slides down his pants.

"Make love to me. You owe it to me," she jokes, but he doesn't laugh. His beautiful face is dark as he mounts her and penetrates her, and his angry lovemaking feels like a punishment. When he's done, he picks up her clothes from the floor and throws them at her.

"Go back and make sure no one sees you. And never, I mean never, return here unless it's a dire emergency."

12

BRIGHT STAR

E mma slips through one of the discrete doors that connect the glitzy passenger quarters to the spartan crew-only areas and takes the narrow metal stairs two at a time, glad she's not wearing high heels. By the time she gets to deck two, six floors down, she's heaving, panting, and swearing to never again indulge in Turkish food.

She joins the dozen people running down the seldom-used second deck. Not much ever happens here, since the ship's bottom is mostly used for storage. But today is not like most days, and Emma has to squeeze between uniforms to get to the center of the action.

The vast storage room crammed with shelves looks like a Home Depot wannabe. Wherever you look, there are shelves loaded with cases, buckets, and boxes, but for the farthest corner, where a body lies on the ground.

Basuki is here already, struggling to fit the plastic mask on the blue face to ventilate. Next to him, Dana looks for IV access, while one of the stretcher team's stewards performs CPR. They're all working feverishly, but just one glance at the body tells Emma that the man has been dead for a while.

The blood has already pooled in the dependent areas, turning the skin into a bruise-like blue, and the neck, where she checks for a pulse, is already cold.

"Stop CPR. He's dead. He's been dead for hours."

The steward stops the chest compressions and steps back.

"That's what I thought." Basuki drops the bag and mask in the Bright Star bag.

"Should I stop too?" Dana asks.

Emma shakes her head.

"No. See if you can get any blood we can test. The captain will want to know. And please check a core temp so we can assess the time of death."

She examines the body. The oily jumper, unzipped to the waist and pulled down his arms to his elbows, tells her he was a mechanic. His open eyes are glazed, his pupils fixed and dilated, and an ugly old scar pulls his lip up in a snarl, uncovering a yellow row of rotten teeth, but there's no pain or fear on his face. If anything, he looks perplexed, and Emma wonders what startled him in his last moments.

He lies supine on his arms that are still caught inside his sleeves. He was getting undressed when he died, Emma guesses, and she wonders why. It's not hot down here.

She palpates his scalp, looking for injuries, but finds nothing. Same with the chest and the back.

"Who found him?" she asks.

"One of the forklift operators."

"Was he lying like this?"

"No. He lay on his face. They turned him to do CPR."

Emma nods. That's what his blue nose says. He died face down and lay like that long enough for the blood to pool in his face.

"Are you done?" The second officer is in charge of security, so he has to take custody of the body and the scene.

Whatever's left of it, after the first responders and everyone else trampled all over it.

"Yes," Emma says.

"The captain wants to see you. Now."

"Lucky me," Emma mumbles. She sighs and heads up the stairs to the navigation deck where Captain Van Huis awaits.

13

THE CAPTAIN

The captain's office on the navigation deck looks the same as it did every other time Emma was summoned here to get berated: the massive mahogany desk with its back to the window is still piled with papers weighed down with antique navigation instruments; the antique charts on the walls still call you to sail to unknown places; and the leather armchair he pointed Emma to is almost as comfortable as those of the Ambrosia and surely better than the wobbly lone chair in her cabin.

Captain Van Huis hasn't changed either. He nods at Emma to come in, then ignores her, as usual, to stick his nose in whatever fascinating paperwork he can't let wait, even though he summoned her so urgently she didn't even get to change. That's why she's still in her black cocktail dress that makes her feel vulnerable, instead of her scrubs and white coat that shield her like armor.

Oops. She forgot her peacock scarf at the Ambrosia. Hopefully Hanna took it. If not, maybe the staff was kind enough to look after it, now that they know her.

She glances at the captain, whose long nose is still stuck into the papers on his desk, wondering what he'd do if she got up and left. She's been here for ten minutes doing precisely nothing, when she should be downstairs, walking Guinness and then getting some sleep before hell breaks loose again. Will it be too late to walk Guinness after I take a shower and get changed, she wonders? Bad enough that I sit here stinking like death. I can't go to Guinness with the smells I must be carting around.

"Dr. Steele."

"Yes."

"Tell me."

"The victim was already long dead by the time he was found, so trying to revive him was futile."

"How do you know?"

"That he was dead?"

"That he'd been dead for a while."

"His skin was already cool to the touch. Blood had pooled in the dependent areas of his body, which, in this case, was his face. And rigor mortis had already started settling in."

"When did he die?"

"I'm not a specialist in forensics, but the general rule of thumb is that the temperature drops by 1.5 degrees every hour. Considering that his core temperature was 92, and we found him at 8 p.m., I'd estimate he died around 4 p.m.. But that's just a rough estimate. There are a lot of variables, including his body weight, the temperature of the area, and his clothing. But because his corneas were clouded and rigor mortis had already developed in the hands, I'd say four hours is pretty close."

"Why did he die?"

"That, I don't know."

"Really? So, for once, you're not suspicious?"

Emma shrugs. "I didn't say that."

"Of course not. Silly me. So, tell me what you think."

"He'll need an autopsy. I didn't find any injuries or signs of violence, but I only did a cursory exam. I'm reasonably sure that he was not shot or stabbed, and his head didn't get bashed in. He may have died of natural causes, like a heart attack or an intracranial hemorrhage, but there are a couple of things that bother me."

"Like what?"

"Like the fact that he was getting undressed when he died. It's not warm down there; why would he get undressed? I thought maybe he needed to urinate, but he had a fly, so he didn't need to get naked for that. Then I wondered if he was planning to have sex."

"Sex? In the storage room?"

Emma doesn't grace him with an answer.

"And, if so, shouldn't his partner have asked for help when she, or he, saw him collapse? Unless they caused it to happen."

"How?"

"I don't know. But one odd thing I noticed was that the little blood Dana managed to get was bright red."

"So?"

"Venous blood is usually dark, especially in dead people, since the cells consume its oxygen."

"What does red blood mean?"

"It could be a sign of cyanide poisoning."

The captain sighs.

"Are you saying someone poisoned him?"

"I'm not saying anything. You asked me what I thought, and I told you."

"So you suspect he went there to have sex with someone and then that person poisoned him with cyanide. Why?"

"I don't know, Captain. Who was the man?"

"He was our best crane operator. A 45-year-old Brazilian, married, three children. Does this help you in any way?"

"No."

"Thank you, Dr. Steele. As always, don't hesitate to stop by if you get any more bright ideas."

14

WALKING GUINNESS

Emma rushes to her cabin to take a shower and scrubs herself twice. When she finally feels clean, she puts on a fresh set of scrubs and checks the time. Almost ten. Hanna goes to bed late, so she might still be up. What if she goes to take Guinness for a quick walk? Just to make sure she's OK?

She feels guilty for having dropped her with Hanna at noon and not seeing her since. Not like she had any time on her hands, but Guinness doesn't know it.

When Emma brought the dog on the ship, she did it mostly out of guilt. She loves her company more than anyone else's, but her present circumstances and obligations make it difficult to look after a dog, even one as low maintenance as Guinness. But when Hanna offered to keep her, excited to have a dog after so long, and Margret, her ex-mother-in-law, told her that the dog seemed forlorn and depressed after Taylor and baby Hope had moved out, Emma thought, *Why not?* So, when the family came to meet her in Istanbul, the opportunity was too good to pass.

But after only half a day on board, Emma already feels guilty. That's nothing new, since feeling guilty and worried is pretty much Emma's normal, but still.

She knocks softly at Hanna's door, hoping to not wake her up. But truth be told, Guinness would hear her anyhow and make enough ruckus to wake up half the ship. But nothing happens. A minute later, Emma knocks again, and Hanna opens the door.

"Emma! Come in!"

"I hate to bother you so late, but I thought I'd take Guinness for a walk."

"She's already gone."

"Gone? Where?"

"For a walk. Archie took her."

Emma's jaw falls.

"Archie? Took Guinness for a walk?"

"Yes. When he brought me back to the cabin after dinner, I mentioned I should take Guinness out, since God only knew when you'd be done with whatever emergency you got called for. He offered to take her for me."

"And you let him?"

Hanna's eyes widen.

"Why not?"

"What if…something happens?"

"Like what?"

"If he mistreats her."

Hanna's mouth drops open.

"Emma, you may not have looked at them carefully, but if there ever were a disagreement between Archie and Guinness, I'd put my money on Guinness. She's got more feet and stronger teeth than he does, or just about any human I know. And why on earth would he mistreat her? He's a charming fellow and a dog lover, and he misses his pup. He was delighted to spend some time with her. Why don't you relax a little? Come in. Let's have a chat and I'll buy you an after-dinner drink. I bet they'll be back in no time."

Emma doesn't really want to chat, but she can use that after-dinner drink, even though she hasn't had much dinner. And she can't go to sleep before knowing that Guinness is safe.

She knows that's silly, and she has no real reason to worry. The fact that the man is an opiate addict doesn't mean he can't be a dog lover and a nice person. But his threats when Emma refused him his fix didn't endear him to her, and he knows Guinness is her dog. Still, he wouldn't hurt her out of spite, would he?

One more reason to wait and make sure she's OK. Emma steps in and takes the glass of Cointreau that Hanna offers her, then drops on her loveseat. Unlike her cramped cabin with its tired furnishings and dirty porthole that wouldn't open, Hanna's cabin is spacious, with comfortable places to sit and a balcony opening on miles and miles of blue sea.

"Cheers." Hanna lifts her glass. "How did your crane man do?"

Emma's jaw falls.

"Crane man?"

"Yes. My steward told me that the crane operator was found down. Isn't that what you got paged for?"

"How did he know?"

Hanna shrugs. "Everyone knows everything about everybody on the ship, especially the stewards. There are no secrets to someone that takes out your trash every day."

Sure there are, Emma thinks. *Like what was that man doing half undressed in the storage room? And why was his blood cherry red?* But that's not something she can discuss with Hanna.

"Did your steward tell you anything about the man?"

"He's been on the ship for just a few months, so he doesn't know him that well, but he said that he was the go-to person if you needed anything."

"Like what?"

"Contraband, I guess. Someone who can procure drugs, alcohol, or other prohibited stuff. You know the ship's a thriving market? You can buy just about anything here. Smartphones, headphones, fancy razors. Also sunglasses, perfumes, and jewelry."

"Stolen?"

"Not necessarily. If there were a wave of thefts on the ship, word would go around and that would be terrible PR for the company. But people forget things — in the dining room, by the pool, or in the cabin when they leave. Sooner or later, all that stuff finds its way to a buyer, and it looks like your patient is the middleman. How is he doing?"

Fortunately, Emma doesn't need to answer. There's a knock at the door and Guinness, dripping with water, bursts in and leaps on Emma. She squeaks like a puppy, gets her soaking wet, licks her face, and spills her drink, all in one smooth move. Hanna laughs.

"Come in, Archie. How did it go?"

"Fabulous, until she jumped into the pool. I tried to hold her back, but she almost pulled me in, so I let her go. She swam a few laps, to the delight of the kids who tried to catch her but couldn't, then came and shook next to me."

Archie opens his arms to show his fancy suit dark with water, and Emma blushes.

"I'm so sorry," she mumbles.

Archie shrugs.

"No worries. That's what dogs do. I should have known better than to take her anywhere near the pool. I had a golden retriever that I always had to drag out of the water, but I didn't know German shepherds were like that too. I'll know better next time."

Emma wants to say there'll be no next time, thank you very much, but Hanna speaks first.

"Good. Let me get you a drink and let's talk about tomorrow."

15

ÇANAKKALE

Emma scratches Guinness behind her ears and tells her what a good girl she was for not eating Archie, though maybe dragging him into the pool wasn't such a bad idea. She promises to take her for a walk early tomorrow morning, then stands to leave.

"Have a good time. Hanna, I'll stop by in the morning to take Guinness out, and I'll try not to wake you up. I…"

"Where are you going?" Hanna asks.

"To sleep."

"Not just yet. Let's figure out what we're doing tomorrow."

"I hope you have a great time, but I have to work."

"Oh, no. Not tomorrow. You know what's tomorrow?"

"Friday?"

"That's not what I'm talking about. Tomorrow is Çanakkale," Hanna says, as if that somehow matters.

Not to Emma. "Oh."

"You know what that is?"

"A port in Turkey, I assume?"

"Not only that. It's the Straight of Dardanelles, and, even more importantly, it's the day we see Troy."

"Troy?"

"Yes. Troy, of the Trojan horse fame? Ancient Troy, immortalized by Homer in the Iliad?"

"Oh. I didn't know it was a real place. I thought it was just fiction."

"Are you kidding? It's real, all right. Even the horse is still there. Tell her, Archie."

"Well, the horse is still there, but it's not the original one. This one was built in 2004 to film the movie with Brad Pitt."

"I'm sorry, I don't think I saw it."

"That's even more of a reason to see it, then." Hanna says. "Tell her, Archie."

Archie glances at Emma with doubt.

"I don't think she's that curious."

"She is, she just doesn't know it. Please tell her."

Archie sighs.

"The Çanakkale stop has a lot to offer. It's the starting point to visit Troy's ruins. It's also the base for the cemeteries at Gallipoli, one of the First World War's most important campaigns. In February 1915, Britain, France, and Russia, the Entente powers, decided to take control of the Ottoman straits. They wanted to bomb Constantinople and cut it off from the Asian Ottoman Empire, but their fleet failed to get through the Dardanelles. Two months later, they attempted an amphibious landing on the Gallipoli peninsula, but after eight months of heavy fighting and extraordinary casualties, they abandoned the campaign. That was a costly failure for everyone, especially Winston Churchill, who was the First Lord of the Admiralty at the time. Gallipoli is a defining moment in Turkish history, since the subsequent fall of the Ottoman Empire established Turkey as a republic under

Mustafa Kemal Atatürk. Gallipoli is also very important in Australia and New Zealand, who had extraordinary casualties in the battle. Anzac Day is when they celebrate their veterans."

"That sounds fascinating, but there's no way I can leave the ship tomorrow. Thank you for thinking of me, though."

"Come on, Emma. Are you really going to miss Troy?" Hanna asks.

"I bet you'll tell me all about it," Emma says, giving Guinness one more pat and heading to the door.

She's glad to get back to her cabin. She turns on the TV, like she always does to sleep, but none of the news channels is working. The movie channel plays *Philadelphia*. Tom Hank's haunted face fills the screen as he dies from AIDS, and, as much as she loves the movie, Emma can't stand to watch it again, so she keeps scrolling. The only other working channel is the ship's channel that runs a recording of the Troy lecture. Dr. Leach looks important, impeccable, and poised.

That should put me to sleep better than the news, Emma thinks, squeezing under her blanket and closing her eyes.

"Let me start with a story you may already know. *The Iliad* is one of the oldest written stories in the world, attributed to Homer and written in verse. It recounts the Mycenaean Greeks' siege of Troy, as they sought to recover Helena, the wife of king Menelaus and the ancient world's most beautiful woman. With help from Aphrodites, the goddess of love, she'd been enticed by young Paris and spirited to Troy. The Greeks came to take her back and revenge the king's honor. *The Iliad* is a story of heroism, pride, and glory. And death.

"After a ten-year long siege without conquering Troy, the Greeks tried a subterfuge. They built a massive wooden horse as homage to the war goddess Athena, left it in front of Troy's gates, and pretended to sail away. Impressed with the magnificent horse, the Trojans brought it inside the city as a monument to their victory. That same night, the Greeks hidden inside it opened the city gates and their comrades destroyed Troy.

"That's just a story, you say. But is it, really? We're about to find out."

His voice is soothing, and he's a good storyteller. *Too bad he's such a jerk*, Emma thinks, before falling asleep.

16

LEILA

B ack in her cabin, Leila finds Ayisha sound asleep. She takes a long, hot shower to wash Selim's love-making off her body as if it soiled her. He's never touched her like that, and his violent rage left her worried and confused.

When they first met on the Columbia University campus years ago, he was the kindest, gentlest, and most considerate man she'd ever met. Not that she'd met many — her high school boyfriend got her pregnant, then enrolled in the army and went to Afghanistan, leaving Leila with a baby in her belly, a soiled reputation, and her family's bitter resentment.

Her father was a pastor. The growing evidence of his daughter's sin made him so angry he couldn't even look at her. Even her mother, an obedient housewife and a pillar of their community, was embarrassed to show her face at social events. Their daughter's pregnancy that couldn't even be fixed with a shotgun wedding had tested her father and humiliated her mother before all their friends, and they couldn't forgive her for it.

Leaving home for college felt like an escape. But going

through school with a baby in tow was not easy. Other girls could let loose and do whatever they wanted. They went out every night and stumbled back drunk in the morning. They slept with whoever they wanted, but still looked at Leila like she had a scarlet letter on her forehead and was too dirty to touch.

Not the boys. They watched her with hungry eyes and stopped to talk to her whenever they met her alone. They came too close and felt free to touch her without asking, since she was already damaged goods.

The first year was awful, and the second was no better until she met Selim. He was so handsome that the girls called him the pirate from *Pirates of the Caribbean*, because he looked like Johnny Depp. But he paid them no mind.

The first time he sat next to her, she imagined it was an accident. The second time, she thought it was a coincidence. But when the other girls started giving her venomous looks, she started wondering if maybe he was interested in her.

But she didn't ask. Between her classes and her evening job as a waitress to pay for lodging, food, and Ayisha's daycare, she had no time to think about men.

The day he asked her out, she stared at him in horror and shook her head. *He doesn't know about the baby,* she thought.

"No. Sorry. I'm too busy," she said, and headed home on the double.

He followed.

"What are you busy with?"

She wanted to tell him that was none of his business, but that would have been rude. So she said, "I'm a single mom. I have a daughter, so I must spend time with her. It's bad enough I'm away most of the day to study and work. I can't leave her behind anymore."

His handsome face lit up from inside when he smiled.

"How about we take her to the park?"

Leila's mouth went dry. It was the first time that someone was willing to spend time with her child.

"Are you serious?"

"Of course. Tomorrow?"

They went to the park, and he bought them ice cream and a red balloon. Leila watched in wonder as they played, Ayisha so delighted she shrieked. For the first time ever, someone other than her showed an interest in her baby, and her heart softened like melted butter.

The weekend after that he took them to the beach. He and Ayisha built sandcastles; then he took her to the water and lifted her above the waves. Leila was trying to study for her programming exam, but she couldn't keep her eyes off them. Seeing her baby happy brought tears to her eyes.

The week after that, he visited them at the studio she rented above a hardware store in Brooklyn. He brought roses, Subway sandwiches, and a stuffed pink dinosaur for Ayisha, and that's when Leila's heart said yes.

He waited for the little girl to fall asleep before taking Leila in his arms and kissing her like nobody had kissed her before, making her insides melt. She wanted him fiercely, but Ayisha was sleeping in her bed, so he left.

When it finally happened, his lovemaking was attentive and meaningful, like he worked on an important project. He first rubbed her tense shoulders, heavy with the weight of the world, then tickled her feet and wiggled her toes, making her laugh. By the time he got to kissing her, she felt like she'd been waiting forever.

"I love you, Leila. More than I can tell. But I have my life's mission to fulfill," he said afterwards.

"What mission is that?" she'd asked, gazing into his loving face and feeling like the luckiest girl in the world.

The passion in his eyes seared her soul.

"I can't tell you, my love. Not yet. But someday I will,

because there's nothing more important to me. Other than you," he had said.

That was years ago. Now they are here to fulfill his life's mission, and just thinking of what she'll have to do raises the hairs on Leila's neck.

Ayisha sighs and coughs, and Leila brings her inhaler.

"There it is, sweetheart. Take a good, deep breath."

"Where is Dad?"

Leila struggles to smile.

"You know we're on this ship to win this contest, so we must pretend we don't know him. But he's fine, and he loves you."

"But he didn't even hug me goodbye."

Leila sighs.

"He will next time, sweetheart. I know he will."

17

ÇANAKKALE

The sky over the Sea of Marmara is putting on a show this morning. As the sun rises toward the horizon, the clouds change from deep purple to red, pink, then gold, so fast Emma can't take enough pictures. I should have taken a video, she thinks, but her companion disagrees.

Guinness is running out of patience. She pulls on the leash, glances back, and wags her tail sideways just enough to make her point.

"Come on now. You said let's go for a walk, and now you're stuck here staring at the sky like it's an all-you-can-eat buffet. There's nothing worth checking out, trust me. I sniffed it thoroughly, and I found nothing. Not a bird, not a squirrel, and most certainly no bacon."

"Sorry," Emma mumbles, putting away her phone and following Guinness, who makes a point of sniffing every inch of the promenade deck. She sticks her nose under doors, sniffs behind the heavy metal cases, and would gladly climb the ladder to the orange safety boats if Emma didn't hold her back. When they meet people, she'd love to stick her black nose between their legs to assess their gender, digestion status, and general health if Emma didn't hold her back. *Wouldn't it be awesome if we had that kind of detector in the ER?* Emma thinks. *A quick sniff, and I'd know if they're sick, sad, or single, and so much more.* She just finished reading a fascinating article about a group of scientists training street dogs to sniff cancers, and feels envious of Guinness's diagnostic acumen, though when the dog gets really serious about sniffing someone, it can get a bit personal. But most people are good sports, and Emma can tell from afar who would rather not get too close to Guinness because they slow down and veer away if they can. They must have had bad experiences with dogs, so they don't want them close, or they're just not dog lovers? Emma has little use for those. She can't sympathize with people who don't like dogs and cats. As for those who abuse them, she can't think of a strong enough punishment.

But it's still early and few people are out on the deck, other than an old smoker who's coughing out his lungs and fouling the air at the stern in the official smoking area, and two sailors going about their morning chores without paying them any mind. The deck is empty, but that won't last long. If Emma wants to exercise Guinness, they'd better get moving before it gets crowded.

"Come on, girl. If you want to walk, let's go."

Guinness wags her tail in agreement and takes three steps before stopping again to explore some invisible clue she's the only one to notice, so Emma takes out her iPhone again. Margret, her ex-mother-in-law, always harasses her for pictures, and Emma does her best to oblige.

She's trying to focus on a colorful boat by the shore when Guinness growls. Emma glances back. A muscular man in shorts and a sweaty T-shirt is jogging behind them.

Good for him, Emma thinks, before recognizing Archie.

Her appreciation vanishes instantly. She pulls Guinness back to make room, but he stops by their side.

"Morning."

"Morning."

Most excited to see him, Guinness tangles her leash around his legs and wags her tail effusively, resisting Emma's efforts to pull her back.

"Go on, please," Emma says, but Archie shakes his head.

"No, thanks. I'm glad for an excuse to stop. Jogging was never my favorite thing, but since I can't resist the buffet, I must do something before it's too late. Last cruise, I gained five pounds in a month. By the end of it I could barely button my coat, and I don't plan to get there again. How about you? How do you stay so slim with all this food?" he asks, and Emma's eyes widen. It's been a long time since anyone called her slim.

"I can thank my pager, I guess. Half the time, I don't get to finish my meals. The other half I eat at the crew mess, and that food won't get you fat."

"Really? How so?"

"You don't have the same temptations you must face at the upstairs buffet. I overeat whenever I eat there. I can't make up my mind, so I try a bit of everything, which ends up being a lot."

"Same here. Sweets are my kryptonite. I can never choose between the bread pudding, the chocolate cake, and the ice cream, so I end up with a plate full of sweets after having had a full meal. I don't love most of them, but I won't know it until I try. And then I feel bad about wasting food when so many people are starving."

Guinness finishes exploring whatever she found, so she moves on, dragging Emma behind. Archie follows.

"Please, don't wait for us," Emma says. "You must need time to prepare for your trip."

Archie shrugs.

"There's no preparing. I'll just throw on some comfortable clothes, pick up Hanna, and head to the bus. I have two hours for that."

"Will you have to lead the cruise passengers through the archeological site?"

"Oh, no. They have local guides for that. But I gave my spiel about Troy yesterday, so I expect some folks will stop by to ask questions. Other than that, I'll just relax, play tourist, and take pictures for my next lecture."

"I hope you enjoy it."

"I certainly will. You won't make it ashore?"

"I seldom do. Company policy requires two medical people on board at all times, in case something happens, so we take turns. With luck, I will occasionally get out, but I have to trade time ashore and have someone cover me. If I do, which ports shouldn't I miss?"

"Petra, for sure. Cairo. And Rhodes."

"Not Alexandria? I've read so much about that library."

"It's all gone. They built a modern one instead, and it's beautiful, but it's only interesting for its architecture. And the city is the pits. Vendors chase you to sell you postcards and fake watches. Fake everything, in fact, from jewelry to designer bags and perfumes. If there's a place in Egypt you should see, it's Cairo. That is a living city with a remarkable history and breathtaking artifacts. If you can, go to the National Museum. It's worth it. But even the city itself is worth seeing."

"Thanks. I'll keep that in mind."

"As for Rhodes, it's one of the most beautiful islands I've ever been to. One of the most breathtaking places, in fact. The blinding white houses and the deep blue sea make it such a typical Greek landscape. It's mesmerizing. I hope someday I get to retire there to spend my days drinking coffee on the balcony and watching the sea. In the evenings, I'd go to the tavern to eat roasted goat, drink retsina, and dance the *sirtaki* with the locals. Where do you plan to retire?"

The question takes Emma by surprise.

"I never thought of that, though I should. Doctors don't last long in my line of business."

"Why not?"

"The stress, I guess."

"Where would you like to live, then? Have you ever been somewhere and told yourself, 'This is where I want to spend the rest of my life?'"

"Falling in love at first sight with a place?"

"Yes."

"I don't think so. I live in northern New York, a stone's throw from Canada. It's peaceful, and Lake Champlain is spectacular, but I don't think I ever fell in love with a place. Actually, that's not true. I fell in love with London, then Paris, then Amsterdam. But none was the love of a lifetime."

"Just one-night stands?"

"More like a fling. I still love going back, but I couldn't live there."

"Neither could I."

"Where do you live?"

"In London."

18

MORNING CLINIC

After their walk, Emma took Guinness back to Hanna's cabin and promised to take her out again at lunch, then got ready for her morning clinic. But throughout her shower and breakfast, she couldn't help but think of Archie. He wasn't the person she expected him to be.

Through her many years in the ER, Emma met hundreds, if not thousands, of addicts. Some were lovely people, some not so much. But even if they got there through no fault of their own, their addiction held them hostage and made them hard to work with because they and Emma were at odds with each other.

They came to the ER to get their fix, and they were miserable without it. Some lashed out in bad ways. Most often against the nurses, who spent more time at the bedside than Emma, but she also got her share of their ire. They wanted nothing else but to get their fix and go, but that went against everything Emma had been taught. *"Primum, non nocere,"* — first, do no harm, said the Hippocratic oath, so giving them something that would reinforce their addiction was a no-no.

She tried to explain, but they didn't care to listen, and they left the ER shouting, cursing, and promising to retaliate. Many did, some didn't, but, in all those years, Emma hadn't seen a single one return acting like a regular person before going through detox.

That's what puzzled her about Archie. His talk about Troy had made it obvious that he was a professional with a knack for telling stories and had a keen sense of humor, but that didn't surprise her. What surprised her was the relaxed way he talked to her this morning, treating her as if she were a real person, not just the miser keeper of his fix.

But then her clinic starts and she has no more time to think about Archie. She's surprised to see a long line of passengers waiting to see her instead of going ashore to admire the famous Trojan horse. *There's no accounting for taste,* Emma thinks, and opens the door to her office.

"This one's a looker," Dana says, dropping a chart on her desk. "Sexy man. Have you seen Johnny Deep in *Pirates of the Caribbean?*"

"I don't think so. I rarely watch movies; I prefer books. Why?"

"He's one of the most handsome men I've ever seen. Just looking in his eyes made me soft in the knees."

Emma chuckles. Dana is smart as a whip and wicked funny, but she has a thing for good-looking men. Sadly, in Emma's experience, handsome men are seldom worth talking to.

"What's he here for?"

Dana frowns.

"His knee, I think? Yes, that's it. He twisted his knee."

Emma nods. "Send him in."

The man limps in, and Emma has to agree with Dana. The man is not tall, but he's movie-set gorgeous, with golden skin and smoldering eyes with black lashes so long they look fake. He gracefully drops into a chair and gives her a dazzling smile.

"Thank you for seeing me, Doctor."

That's unusual too. People rarely thank her for seeing them, since they know she gets paid for it.

"Of course. What can I help you with?"

"My knee."

"What about it?"

"I must have twisted it last night when I left the cocktail party. You know how it goes — you get a drink, then a second, then a third, and then you're ready to boogie even if you're not a dancer. This morning when I tried to stand my knee wouldn't cooperate. It felt so loose I had to grab a cane."

Emma wonders where on the ship he found a cane to grab. The ship's stores are full of expensive watches, diamond jewelry, and fragrances. They even keep snacks, toothpaste, and anti-fungal shampoo in a well-hidden cupboard, but canes? Not so much. But she doesn't get to ask.

"Can you help me, please? I'm so disappointed I couldn't go ashore to see Troy. That was the highlight of the trip for me. Can you get me better?"

Emma smiles.

"Let's see what we can do."

His medical history is unremarkable. So is the first part of the exam. The knee is not red, hot, or swollen — all signs of infection, or at least inflammation. She decides to test the ligaments by checking its stability.

"Where are you from?" Emma asks, looking into his eyes while stabilizing the thigh with one hand and pulling the leg forward with the other. The ACL, the anterior cruciate ligament, is tight, as it should be.

"London. Have you been there?"

"Of course. One of the most amazing cities in the world. I love everything about it. The art, the theaters, and even the food," Emma says, holding on to the thigh and pushing the leg back to check his posterior cruciate ligament. That one works fine too. The man smiles.

"Everything but the traffic. Isn't the food something? Not long ago, we had nothing but overcooked vegetables and bland Sunday roasts. But now you can find anything — Chinese, Indian, Arabic, Thai — whatever your heart fancies. What's your favorite?"

Emma pretends to be thinking as she pushes the knee outward. The ligament feels tight, and the patient shows no sign of discomfort, she notes in her mind.

"I'm partial to Thai. I spent a few months in Thailand, so Thai food reminds me of those wonderful days. But I can't eat it spicy like they do — not even close. I wonder if it's genetics, or if they teach children to eat spicy at a very young age. What do you think?"

He shrugs. "I don't know. I've never been that far east."

"What's your favorite food?" Emma looks into his eyes as she pushes the leg inwards to test his LCL. He smiles back.

"Arabic, I guess. Have you ever had hummus?"

"Are you kidding? I like hummus, but I love tabuleh even more."

His face lights up. "I do too. That mouth-watering combination of parsley with tomatoes and lemon? Fresh and delightful. Especially with hot, crispy falafel."

Emma lets go of his leg.

"The knee doesn't look bad, but I'd be careful if I were you, especially when climbing stairs. How about a knee brace for support, and taking it easy for a day or two? See you back in two days?"

The man nods as his eyes slide around the room, taking in the cabinets full of pills, the slit lamp, and the locked controlled substance cabinet.

"Thank you so much, Dr. Steele. Great meeting you. How about drinks tonight?"

19

THE PUNCHING BAG

When Emma heads back to her cabin after clinic, she's still wondering why Sexy Man, as Dana dubbed him, came to see her. His knee couldn't have been better if it was brand new. He forgot to limp as he strutted out of her office, and he even left his cane behind. So why did he come?

Emma didn't flatter herself that he came to see her. He wanted something, but what? Drugs, most likely. He thought he'd sweet-talk her into giving him something. But then why hadn't he asked?

She checked her watch. She had just enough time to get changed and head up to the gym for her training, so she hustled.

A few months ago, after she'd helped Antonio get released by the Japanese police and clear his name of the murder they suspected, he had offered to give her Muay Thai classes in thanks.

"Listen, Emma, don't take this the wrong way, but I've never met someone more prone to getting themselves into sticky situations. Not sure how you managed to stay alive until now, most likely through sheer luck, but how about I teach you a few moves? Just in case you find yourself in trouble again? It's excellent exercise, too. It will help tone you up and drop a few pounds."

Emma laughed so hard she almost choked.

"No wonder you can't find a woman, if that's how you woo them," she'd said.

Antonio had stared at her with wide eyes, wondering if she'd gone crazy. A woman was the last thing he needed, and Emma laughed even harder.

"Just kidding," she said, wiping her eyes. "That's very kind of you, but I'm afraid I can't afford your training rates. I'm not a rich tourist; I just work on the ship, like you do, and your classes would make me bankrupt."

Antonio shook his head.

"I'm not talking about you booking classes. I'll do it in my free time as a thank you for helping me out. If it weren't for you, I'd be rotting in some Japanese jail."

Emma accepted. Since then, she'd been spending an hour a week getting the shit beat out of her. But, strangely enough, she enjoyed it.

Punching and kicking helps her vent her anger — and God knows she has plenty of that. Every time her fists or her feet hit the bag, the crust of old ice around her heart gets fractionally thinner. Because for as long as she can remember, Emma has been filled with a rage she never expressed, but she never let go.

It started with her mother, who used to beat little Emma until she peed herself and fell to her knees to beg for mercy. After she grew and refused to beg, Mother decided that the beatings had lost their efficiency. That's when she chopped her hair so short that patches of pink scalp shone through. Grandma had cried and tried to stop her, but she couldn't. The kids at Emma's school laughed at her for months.

The ice around her heart got even thicker when Victor left her for another woman. To top it off, Taylor blamed Emma for it and poisoned her life with her nasty moods. That all made it hard for Emma to allow anyone inside her heart, no matter how lonely she felt.

She never knew why until Antonio recognized it as rage.

Letting her anger loose helped her breathe better. Emma had never cared for therapy — too much talk, too much bullshit, and way too personal. But beating the crap out of that bag? That, she could do.

Antonio held the bag, watching Emma dance on her feet and throw jab after jab.

"Not from the shoulder. From the core! That's it. One more. Good. Now jab and cross. Always from the core."

She jabbed her right fist into the bag, then pivoted and threw a cross with her left. Jab-cross, jab-cross.

"Knees soft. Drop your shoulders. The work shouldn't come from your shoulders. They're too wimpy to give you enough power. The power comes from the big muscles of your torso: the back, the abdomen, and the chest. Get them working, will you?"

Jab-cross. Jab-cross. Emma thought of her mother sending her to the backyard to cut a switch from a tree. It had to be thin and flexible enough to wrap around her body like a whip, but not flimsy enough to break after a few lashes. She then had to remove her underwear and bend over a chair so that Mother wouldn't strain her back.

Mother would check the twig, and a loving smile spread across her face.

"Turn around," Mother said, taking off Emma's glasses to make sure they didn't get damaged.

"Mother, please. I'm so sorry. I won't do it again," Emma heard herself say, her teeth chattering like she was freezing. But she wasn't cold. Just terrified.

Mother smiled.

"I'll make sure of that. Turn around now."

"Mother, don't. Please don't. I'll be better. I'll be a better daughter. I swear! Please, please don't."

She dropped to her knees and hugged Mother's legs, keeping close enough for her not to strike. After all, she wouldn't hurt herself, would she?

Mother loved that. Her eyes twinkled, and she sighed with fake regret at seeing Emma beg.

"How many times have you said that already? I'm afraid it's too late. It's time for you to learn your lesson."

"But I learned it, Mother, I swear," Emma lied, choking on her tears and her fear. But Mother knew. She always knew.

"Turn around now, or you'll get double."

Double? Double what? Emma wondered. She never knew there was a dose. No matter how long it took, Mother didn't stop until Emma peed herself. And, to make sure that didn't happen too soon, she always sent her to the bathroom first.

Jab-cross. Jab-cross. Kick.

"Wow. That was something," Antonio says. "That's enough for today."

Emma looks around to discover she's in the little training room by the gym, not in her mother's old kitchen. And she's a grown woman, not the terrified eight-year-old she remembered. She's panting, dripping with sweat, and she's shaking so hard she can barely stand, but Antonio stares at her like he found a treasure.

"When you hit that bag, what were you thinking about? What was going through your mind?"

"I was thinking about my mother."

20

LUNCH

The best part of Emma's martial arts training is having lunch with Antonio afterward. Once freed from the burden of her fury, she's exhausted but light, inside and out. And Antonio is fun to be with.

The Oceanview buffet is almost empty today. All those who could, passengers or crew, went to see Troy and won't be back until the evening, so Emma and Antonio get seats at one of the coveted outdoor tables which are rarely available. From up here, they have a bird's-eye view of the restless blue sea down below.

How wonderful it must be to fly, Emma thinks, sitting to hold the table as Antonio goes to get drinks. The breeze ruffles her hair and her skin prickles as the sweat dries down her back, and she wishes she'd gone to shower first. She probably stinks, and she's a bit embarrassed about the performance she put up in front of Antonio, but she also feels strangely liberated. It's like more of the ice wall surrounding her heart has melted. Who knows? With luck, she may become an ice-free person someday, with feelings she allows herself to feel.

Antonio returns with a tray full of drinks, and Emma bursts into laughter. She never forgets to tell her patients to keep hydrated, but this is over the top. He gives her a quizzical look as he sets three glasses in front of her and keeps one for himself.

"This is water for hydration. This is fruit juice for sugar and vitamins. And this is chamomile tea to help you relax."

Emma frowns.

"I don't need to relax. And I hate chamomile."

"Don't drink it then. So, speaking about your performance…"

"I don't want to talk about it."

He doesn't seem to hear.

"Speaking about your performance. Quite remarkable, I might add. Reminds me of myself. I was only seven when my step-uncle Joe taught me about sex. I wasn't yet into sex at that time, so I can't say I enjoyed it. But, when I eventually grew up, thinking about my uncle Joe helped me become who I am today, an MMA champion and all. Anger is a powerful motivator. It can also poison your heart if you don't learn to channel it right. With all due respect, I think you're too old to become a professional fighter, but with some training, you could get in the best shape of your life. And learn to fight like I've seldom seen a woman fight."

He goes quiet and sips on his water while Emma lets this sink in. It takes her a while, and when she finally opens her mouth to speak someone beats her to it.

"Look at that! Two of my favorite people. How are you guys doing?"

Nok hugs them, then drags a chair from the next table and sits between them and shakes her head, letting the wind ruffle her dark locks. She looks as beautiful as ever, even in a worn-out T-shirt and a pair of skimpy shorts, but there are new wrinkles between her brows.

"We're good here," Antonio says. "Emma just had one of her best training sessions yet. I didn't know I had such a talent on my hands, but now I do. How are you, Nok?"

That's when Emma realizes she has never seen them together. And why would she? Nok, who's seldom on the ship, is the captain's wife, and Antonio is his lover. What a lucky man, Captain Van Huis! Emma can't imagine what these two amazing people find in him, but she has no room to judge.

Nok sighs.

"Did you hear the news?"

"What news?"

"There's a major political crisis brewing. It appears that Hamas has orchestrated an unexpected incursion in Israel. In a few hours, they left behind thousands of dead and kidnapped hundreds of hostages into Gaza. Israel is expected to retaliate. The whole Middle East is on fire, and the Red Sea is a terrible place to be."

Antonio shrugs. "That happened before, and nothing came of it. It won't be any different this time."

Nok shakes her head. "I hope you're right, but I'm worried. So is Pieter. He's on the phone with the company, right now, looking at changing our itinerary to keep the ship safe. They're talking about skipping all the ports in Israel and heading straight to Petra. I hope they don't skip Egypt. I've been looking forward to seeing the pyramids."

21

BLACKMAIL

It's past noon. It's eerily quiet, and not a cloud mars the sky as I lie in my comfortable teak chair on the upper deck. Unlike the promenade deck downstairs, where people never stop walking and talking, and the sailors keep scraping and painting like a speck of rust will doom the ship, here on the upper deck I'm all alone, surrounded by an army of empty chairs.

I roll my blanket and slide it under my head, acting like I'm just reading my book and minding my business, but I'm not. Over it, I'm watching the bridge with its comings and goings, trying to make sense of their pattern.

A tall young man in an ironed white shirt passes by with a stack of papers. I watch him discreetly as he slips inside through an unmarked metal door.

I'll check it later, I tell myself and get back to my book when I hear heavy steps behind me. A pair of steel-toed boots stops by my side.

"Artsy?"

I look up. It's a mechanic in a soiled jumper. He's short

and brown, with dark curly hair shining like it's oiled, and he carries a bucket. Paint, by the smell.

"I'm afraid you got the wrong person."

He shakes his head.

"Don't think so. Remember Jacopo?"

Do I remember Jacopo? he asks, and the hair rises on my back.

"I don't think so," I lie.

"That's too bad. You may or may not know it, but he died last night. They think it was a heart attack. Maybe. Or maybe not. But you owe me some money."

"I do?"

"Yes. Remember the deal? 35K when you saw your box on the ship. The other 35 when you got it back. No stowaways, no drugs. Remember now?"

Well then. That's a surprise, and not a nice one. I didn't think that stupid man would want to share the money, but he must have talked to this guy, whoever this is. I was wrong, and now I'm in trouble. Big trouble.

"Let's say that I do. Who wants to know?"

"Since my roommate died, I'll take over the job. I'll look after your box and get it delivered in Dubai. That will be 50K today and another 50K at the end."

I struggle to smile. Even if I wanted to pay him — and I don't — I don't have that kind of money.

"We agreed on 35K, not 50. And I already gave Jacopo the money."

"That would be unfortunate, because I looked everywhere and I couldn't find it. But I don't think you did. I think you stiffed him, possibly in more ways than one. Still, that's not the point. The point is that I get my 50K, or I tell security about your box. And if I do, no matter what's in it, you won't get it back."

"That would be most regrettable."

"It would, wouldn't it? We wouldn't want that to happen. That's why you'll bring me my money tonight. Ten minutes to midnight, the third deck, at the stern."

I gather every shred of honesty I can muster and look him straight in the eye.

"Listen, man. What's your name?"

"Call me Rajiv."

"Listen, Rajiv, I don't have that kind of money on me. As I told you, I gave Jacopo the 35K. Where do you imagine I can find another 50 on this ship before midnight? I can't. I need a few days."

A shadow of doubt crosses his dark face. He's not sure if I'm lying, but what I said makes perfect sense. It also happens to be true. I surely don't have 50K sitting under my mattress.

"Give me a few days. I'll make some phone calls, and I'll get the money sent over. I might be able to pick it up in Rhodes, but there's no way I can get it before."

His greedy little eyes search my face, looking for the truth, and I look him straight in the eye.

"I don't have 50K, I swear," I say, and I cross myself.

"OK then. The night after Rhodes. Same time, same place."

"Where can I find you if there's a problem?"

"Make sure there's no problem. And you don't need to find me. I'll find you."

I watch him leave, banging the bucket against his leg, imprinting his figure into my mind.

I have three days to come up with a plan and execute it. And I need to make it look like an accident. The last thing I need is for the ship's security to tighten now. I watch Rajiv get out through the same unmarked door as the young officer. I count to ten; then I follow.

22

A SAD CHILD

After saying goodbye to Nok and Antonio, Emma went to take Guinness out for a walk. The dog thought it was a swell idea, so they headed to the promenade deck, which is so empty it looks abandoned. It's like they have the entire ship to themselves.

Walking round and round the same few hundred yards of narrow deck would bore most people to death, Emma thinks, but not Guinness. Every time they pass the exact same spot they passed ten minutes ago, she still finds some other news to sniff. Her black nostrils flare as she pulls the secretly scented air up her long snout, analyzes it, and expresses her expert opinion by raising her hackles to make herself look bigger, angling her ears from vertical to the horizontal helicopter worried look, or changing her tail's position and the rhythm of its wag.

There's one spot where she never fails to growl as she sniffs under a heavy metal door to some place inside that's not allowed to passengers, and Emma wonders what she senses. If she had to bet, she'd guess there's a cat on board. *That would be fun,* Emma thinks, remembering what she read about Simon, the Royal Navy's best mouser and the only cat recipient of the Dickin Medal, the animals' Victoria Cross. "During the battle, Simon was gravely wounded and he barely survived injuries from an artillery shell. But despite his weakened condition, his behavior was of the highest order. He raised the ship's morale by killing off hundreds of rats and thus staving off an infestation," his commendation said. *And some people think animals are only good for meat,* Emma thinks, watching Guinness study the same fire extinguisher for the fifth time.

A couple more laps, and the dog seems to have had enough, so Emma takes her back to Hanna's cabin for a nap. Guinness is a fan of long, frequent naps. *That's how she maintains her youthful looks,* Emma thinks, and considers doing the same.

She stops by Medical, where Dana, who's on first call, is filing charts, printing invoices, and calling back the patients they saw yesterday to make sure they're doing alright.

"All good?" Emma asks.

"Yep. Except for the little girl."

"What little girl?"

"The little girl with asthma you saw yesterday. She was supposed to come for a recheck this morning, but she didn't. I called their cabin three times and got no answer."

"They must have gone ashore."

Dana shrugs.

"Maybe. Though I wonder what a child like that would do an entire day in the heat with nothing but rocks to look at.

"Good point. What's their cabin number?"

"735."

"I'll go check on her."

"Thanks, Emma."

"Sure."

I can't go to a sick child empty handed, Emma thinks, so she takes the elevator to the Oceanview Buffet and grabs a cup to get her ice cream. What would she like? Chocolate, for sure. And strawberry maybe? She adds some chocolate syrup, steals a spoon, then rushes down the stairs to deliver it before it melts.

Cabin 735 is on the left. Emma rings the doorbell, then knocks at the door, but nobody answers. She knocks again. Still nothing. She's wondering if she should use her masterkey to get in, when the door cracks open.

"Who is it?"

"I'm Dr. Steele. I came to see how Ayisha is doing."

"Oh, Dr. Steele. She's doing fine, thanks," her mother says, but doesn't open the door.

"May I see her? I brought her something."

The woman hesitates, then opens the door to allow Emma in.

Wearing a pair of pink pajamas with scattered white lambs, her curly dark caught in a pink bow, Ayisha sits on the loveseat by the window, clutching her pink dinosaur. Her breathing seems fine, but she looks so sad that Emma feels worried.

"Look what I brought you." She lifts the cup with the softened ice cream. The brown and the pink have melted into each other, mingling into a swirly deep mud, but Ayisha doesn't seem to mind. Her round eyes stay glued to Emma.

"For me?"

"Yep. I don't know what your favorite flavor is, so I brought you mine. Chocolate and strawberry. And here's a spoon."

Ayisha glances at her mother, asking for permission. The mother nods.

"But sit at the table; otherwise, the entire cabin will be nothing but chocolate," she says.

She scoops the pile of papers and the open laptop sitting

on the table to make room, and drops them on the bed. Emma glances at the screen, which shows some kind of electronic circuit.

"Are you working?" Emma asks.

The woman slams the laptop closed.

"Just catching up on some stuff."

"What do you do?"

"I work in IT."

"Where?"

"Oh, here and there. I freelance."

It's obvious that she doesn't want to talk to her, but Ayisha seems to really enjoy her ice cream. She thoroughly licks every spoon, keeping her eyes on Emma.

"Thank the nice lady doctor for bringing you ice cream, Ayisha."

"Thank you."

"Sure. What's your favorite flavor, so I know what to bring you next time?" Emma asks.

"Chocolate," Ayisha says.

"Oh, but there's no need to bother. She doesn't want to eat a lot of ice cream because it's not good for her teeth, is it, Ayisha?"

The child nods, but her sad eyes stay glued to Emma, who feels not only dismissed but also dis-invited to return. She wonders why. Most passengers love attention. Before today, Emma has never stopped by a patient's cabin without being invited to sit and offered whatever they had, if only water. Extricating herself afterward is always a challenge, but not today. This woman doesn't want her here and she can't wait for Emma to be gone.

"Very good. You guys come by Medical or give us a call if there's any problem, OK?"

The woman nods and opens the door.

"Come back," Ayisha says.

23

RHODES

Two days later, Emma woke up more excited than a kid on Christmas morning. They'll be in Rhodes today, and, wonder of wonders, she scored a rare treat: a shore excursion. That means she'll be chaperoning a passenger tour, and she'll get to see everything that passengers pay $200 for without paying a dime. Sure, she'll have to make sure nobody gets lost or hit by a car while crossing the street, but it's worth it. She hasn't stepped ashore since Istanbul because she let Dana take the whole day in Izmir and covered Basuki's clinic, so they promised to cover for her today.

She walked Guinness at dawn and told her the good news. The dog cocked her head to listen, and wagged her tail politely to congratulate her, but she was much more interested in the smells. *It's only fair*, Emma thought, and went back to her cabin to get ready.

She decided on the lemon-colored summer dress she'd bought in Istanbul, put on her sturdy walking sandals, and grabbed her sunglasses. She dropped her sun hat and a bottle of water in her brown messenger bag and took off.

They're meeting in the showroom, where the passengers get grouped by destination before being dispatched to their respective buses. Emma's ticket says 4D, The Best of Lindos, Acropolis, and Rhodes town with lunch. Other than lunch, she doesn't know any of those, but she's so eager to get off the ship she'd welcome a freak show if that was on offer.

She sits in the last row of the showroom, a glitzy affair in burgundy velvet and gold, and studies her charges for the day. She waves to a few old patients before noticing that Dana's Sexy Man is in her group, and she wishes he wasn't.

The day she saw him in clinic and he invited her for a drink, Emma told him politely that she did not go out with patients. Not only was it against her principles, but company policy prohibited the crew from fraternizing with guests, so she had to decline. She hasn't seen him since, but she's not comfortable around him. She still doesn't know why he came to see her in clinic, but she's sure it wasn't for his knee, and that makes her wary.

Oh well. It is what it is, she tells herself. There'll be forty people on that bus, so what are the chances he'll end up anywhere near her?

When their number gets called, Emma stays behind to make sure that all those on her tour heard the announcement before following them to the bus.

"Thirty-two," she tells the guide, a small woman with a very authentic Greek nose and wing-like dark eyebrows who wears a distracting orange baseball cap with a propeller. The woman nods.

"Make sure we have everyone every time we get back to the bus," she says.

Emma walks to the back of the bus where she has two seats to herself and sits by the window, exhilarated to be off the ship. The bus takes off, and the guide starts talking.

"Morning, everyone. My name is Sophia, and I will be

your guide today as we visit Rhodes, one of Greece's most popular islands. The most beautiful one, if you ask me, but I'm born here, so I may not be completely impartial. We'll start with a scenic drive of 30 miles along the coast to the town of Lindos. On the way, we'll stop to see the spot where the famous Colossus of Rhodes, one of the Ancient World's Seven Wonders, used to stand watch over the harbor. The Colossus was a bronze statue of Helios, the Greek sun god. He was 120 feet tall, almost as tall as the Statue of Liberty, which is 151 feet tall. Most sources call her 305 feet, but that includes her 154-foot pedestal. The Colossus stood watch above the harbor for only a short time, because an earth-quake toppled it after a few years. Today's replacement, though majestic, is just a recent reconstruction.

"In Lindos, we will take the steep path to the ancient Acropolis towering above the town. Please be advised that we'll have a serious climb, including lots of stairs. If you have mobility problems, you may choose to stay in town and shop, wander through the city's old cobbled lanes, or enjoy a coffee or cold drinks at one of the many cafes. Alternatively, you can hire a donkey to take you up part of the way to the Temple of Athena Lindia that looks down on St Paul's Bay. It's named for Saint Paul, who, in AD 51, came to the island to preach Christianity."

"Hi."

Emma turns her eyes from the mesmerizing sea down below. Sexy Man leans above her, dazzling her with his smile.

"Hello."

"May I sit with you?"

Emma looks for an excuse, but other than "I've got cooties" nothing else comes to mind, so she picks her bag and puts it in her lap.

"Good to see you," he says, spreading himself in the seat and invading Emma's space.

"Yes," she says. "How's your knee?"

"Much better, thank you. You were right. A bit of rest, and it's as good as new."

"Excellent."

She turns back to the window, hoping he'll take the hint, but no.

"How long have you worked on cruise ships?"

"Just a few months."

"Don't you love it? Seeing all these awesome places, and meeting interesting people, all while doing your job? I wish I was that lucky."

Emma forces a smile.

"What do you do?"

"I'm an engineer. Give me a pump or a panel, and I'm happier than a pig in shit."

Emma can't help but laugh.

"Are you enjoying your cruise?"

"Very much. It has its challenges, but all in all, it's quite the experience."

Emma wants to ask him about the challenges, but the bus stops at the fake Colossus and everybody gets off to take pictures.

Ten minutes later, she waits for everyone to get aboard before coming in to count them. They're all there, even Sexy Man who occupies the seat next to her, and Emma isn't sure how she feels about it.

"By the way, my name is Selim. What's yours?"

"I'm Emma."

"Good to meet you, Emma. You travel alone?"

Emma laughed.

"I work on the ship, remember?"

"I do. Are you single?"

Emma wonders how to tell him in no uncertain terms that her relationship status is none of his business when the bus stops again. They've arrived at Lindos.

Fortunately, the guide doesn't need her to watch those who stay downtown but wants her to keep an eye on those who pay a handful of euros to hire a mule to take them uphill.

Emma can't help but feel bad watching the tiny animals with soulful eyes buckling under the weight of the well-fed tourists who prefer to sit in the awkward saddle, their feet dangling close to the ground, rather ride than climb the hill on their own two feet. The placid mules flick their tails to smack the flies as they take careful steps up the steep dusty road, following their owners who lead them by their reins.

"It doesn't look pretty, but both the mules and their owners need to eat. And the mules who don't work end up as *loukaniko*. That's Greek sausage."

It's Selim, of course. Emma picks up the pace, hoping to leave him behind, but then she remembers she's supposed to shepherd the tourists and slows down to a crawl. Selim sticks by her side, and once again, she wonders what he wants from her.

"Are you the only doctor on board?"

"No. There's a crew doctor, too."

"And how many nurses?"

"Three." Emma says, wondering why he cares.

"Is there a pharmacist?"

That's definitely getting weird, Emma thinks, and she turns around.

"Excuse me, I have to go see what's going on with those two."

She heads to a couple of guests she's seen in clinic.

"How are you doing? How's your cough?"

"Much better, thanks."

She stays with them, hoping Sexy Man finds someone else to pester. Sure enough, when they finally reach the top, he's nowhere to be seen.

24

GREEK LUNCH

J ust as the guide promised, the views from the top are magnificent. Standing between the slender marble columns that the years baked into the soft yellow of acacia honey, Emma can see the entire village of Lindos spreading down below, looking like it's made from Lego bricks, all blinding white. The houses are square and flat-roofed, all but the octagonal church covered in terracotta tiles. Beyond it, the sea is dreamy blue, soothing the eyes and the soul. Behind the promontories that hug the waves like loving arms, the mountains stand velvety purple. There's so much beauty that Emma's heart feels full.

The others feel it too. They ooh and ahh, stumbling on the uneven ground to take pictures and climbing up the walls to take selfies. Emma worries they'll tumble and crash into the precipice, hundreds of feet below when, like a worried mother hen, the guide gathers them around her.

"This is the famous Acropolis of Lindos. It's 2500 years old and was fortified successively by the Greeks, the Romans, the Byzantines, the Knights of St. John, and the Ottomans.

There are so many layers to unearth that even the archeologists have trouble interpreting where the remains come from. Here you can see the Doric Temple of Athena Lindia, built on the site of an earlier temple.

"That is the Sanctuary's Propylaea, the monumental gateway separating the secular and religious areas of the city. Down by the steps to the acropolis, cut straight into the rock, you'll find the relief of a Rhodian trireme, an ancient galley with three banks of oars used by the ancient maritime civilizations of the Mediterranean.

"Those two towers are all that's left from the Castle of the Knights of St. John, which was built before 1317 to follow the cliff's shape. There's so much to see here. Still, the thing most tourists ask about it is whether this is where Anthony Quinn's movie, *The Guns of Navarone*, was made. And the answer is yes."

The trip down is easier, and no mules are involved. Emma glances left and right, looking for Sexy Man, but he seems to have vanished, and that worries her. Like it or not, he's one of her charges, so it's her job not to leave him behind.

She reassures herself that he probably had enough of the climb and turned around to stay in the village where they will meet at the Goat's Head taverna for lunch before taking the bus to Rhodes town.

The restaurant doesn't look big from outside, but once you pass through the dark hallways into the bright inner yard, dozens of tables covered in white and blue checkered tablecloths line up in long rows. The guests follow the guide to the long table, which is already set with plates, glasses, and white wine carafes; choose their seats; and head to the buffet.

Emma finds a seat at the quiet end of the table. She loved the tour, but she feels over-socialized. She hasn't talked, smiled, and mingled so much in ages, and she feels an acute need for peace.

She waits for everyone else to return to the table with their overfilled plates before heading to the buffet to get food. It all looks delicious, other than the spanakopita, that evil spinach pastry she only tried once. She loads her plate with olives, some shiny green ones and some wrinkly black, stuffed grape leaves topped with sour cream, and souvlaki, a skewer with bite-sized cubes of grilled meat whose smell makes her mouth water. *I just hope it's not mule,* she thinks.

"Try the moussaka. It's excellent," a voice says, and Emma worries that Sexy Man is back. But it's Archie, who just appeared out of nowhere,

"Where are you coming from?"

"From Rhodes old town. I went to the archeological museum to say hi to a couple of old friends and see if they found anything new. You?"

"The acropolis."

"Oh, isn't it beautiful?"

"Amazing. Almost as beautiful as the scenery surrounding it," Emma says.

Archie shakes his head and puts two stuffed grape leaves on his plate.

"Spoken like a true tourist. If you were even an aspiring archeologist, you'd know there's nothing more beautiful than rocks."

"How about bones?"

"You have a point. Where are we sitting?"

Emma laughs.

"I don't know about you, but I sit there."

"Good enough." He takes the seat next to hers. "How was your morning?"

"Stupendous. You were right."

"Of course I was. About what?"

"About Rhodes being so incredibly beautiful. I can see how you fell in love with it."

"I have it in my blood. *Stin ygeiásas,*" he says, touching his glass to hers.

The wine is light and rough, but it smells like grapes and goes well with the food.

"It's not exactly a grand cru, but it will have to do," Archie says. "What are you doing this afternoon?"

"Going to the Rhodes' old town, to see the Grand Masters' palace. Is it nice?"

Archie shrugs.

"It's a fake. They built an Italian fascist construction on the site of a ruined Ottoman palace that replaced a fortress of the Knights Hospitaller built on top of a Byzantine Citadel erected above the ruins of an ancient temple dedicated to Helios. I could give you more details, but it would give you a headache. I get one every time I see it, so I avoid it like the plague. Mussolini's name is still on a plaque by the entrance."

"What does Mussolini have to do with anything?"

"Fascist Italy occupied Rhodes, and many other Greek islands, during the Second World War. Then 1947's Treaty of Peace with Italy declared that the Italians should return the Dodecanese Islands to Greece, which converted the palace into a museum that's a major money-maker for Rhodes."

"Oh," Emma said, feeling disappointed.

"Mind you, it's an archeologist's nightmare, but the tourists like it. You probably will too. It has tons of marble and mosaics, and, for a fake, it's well done."

When Emma returned to her bus and was glad to find that Sexy Man had reappeared, but he'd vacated the seat next to her, and Emma wondered if she'd offended him. But it felt good to be alone.

As Archie had said, the castle was a disappointment, but the Street of the Knights and its medieval buildings with emblazoned facades made up for it. She had half an hour to shop, so she bought herself a pair of handmade Roman sandals made of soft leather that cradled her legs and bought Margret a mug with a scowling painted owl. It was far from pretty, but it was expensive enough to be authentic. And Margret loved owls.

25

AN UNPLEASANT TASK

I'm done eating, but I can't bring myself to return to my windowless cabin, so I sit at a table by the pool nursing my iced tea and watch the tourists make fools of themselves. Tonight is barbecue night, so they crowd around the grills like they haven't eaten in a week and stuff themselves with more meat than we used to eat in a month when I was home. After a few blissful minutes of silence, the band starts playing again, so loud I can't hear myself think, and I've had it. I head to my cabin for a nap before taking care of Rajiv. I must do it before he takes care of me. Fortunately, I found what I needed in Lindos. My plan is not ideal, but it will do. It should buy me a few days before they figure out that his passing wasn't God's wish.

I wait until midnight, when all the fuss outside quiets, then sneak out of my cabin in a pair of dark shorts and a hoodie. If anyone wonders where I'm going, I look like an insomniac going for a walk on the promenade deck.

But I'm not going for a walk. I head down to the second deck, where the crew cabins are. Thanks to my new friend, the doctor, I have a universal key that should let me open any door on the ship. Maybe? Not sure it would let me inside the bridge, but it should surely let me into some poor slob's cabin.

Once on the third deck, I wave my key over the door to Medical, and it clicks open. I step into the sterile hallway and put on the blond wig and the glasses I hid inside my hoodie. One minute later, I exit through the other door, the one opening to the crew quarters, looking nothing like my usual self. At first, I was confused to see two different doors labeled Medical, one toward the passengers' side and another one towards the crew quarters, but then I saw the potential. That gives me a smooth way to pass from one side of the ship to the other and back without facing the cameras.

I head down the hallway to the stairs, then down to the second deck and turn the opposite way from the storage room where Jacopo found his peace. And here I am, in the crew quarters, with its hundreds of cabins no bigger than a freezer, each set up for two.

Rajiv said Jacopo was his roommate. I bet they didn't replace him and he's still alone in his cabin. If he's not, I'll have to sneak out quietly and think of another plan.

There it is. I put on my surgical gloves and wave the doctor's key over the lock. The click sounds so loud it startles me, but the loud snoring inside doesn't stop.

I aim my penlight at the upper bunk. It's empty. Good. I grab the washcloth with the vial from the zip bag, I crush it, and press it over Rajiv's face, holding my breath.

His eyes pop out and he struggles to escape, but I've got him in a neck lock. I count to five and he goes limp. I let go of him and drop the washcloth back into the zip bag, seal it, and put it in my pocket.

Now to the less pleasant part.

I roll him to his side and pull down his shorts. *His skinny ass is hairier than a monkey's,* I think, as I spread his cheeks to find the hole.

I really hate to touch my clothes with that hand, but I must. I grab the other zip bag, the one with the syringe. Thank God for zip bags and plastic gloves, I think, and I stick the plastic catheter inside the man and push the plunger all the way.

For a few seconds, I press his butt cheeks together to make sure nothing comes out, then pack the syringe and put the bag back in my pocket. I'll have to throw this hoodie overboard.

I pull up his shorts and cover him to the neck, then glance around his cabin for anything of interest. I'm not looking for anything in particular, but I need to wait and make sure he doesn't wake up before my little gift starts working.

His iPhone is on the charger. I try to turn it on, but it doesn't recognize me. *How unfortunate,* I think, and show it Rajiv's face. It opens like magic.

I glance at his messages, looking for someone he's close to, but there are way too many, and most are in a language I don't recognize. Oh well.

I type: "Sorry, you all. I just couldn't take it anymore," and plant the phone in his hand, making sure his fingerprints show in all the right places, then let it drop on his bed.

It's been a few minutes, and nothing's happening. I wonder if I miscalculated the dose when a big shiver goes through him, but he doesn't open his eyes. Good enough. I can't stay here one minute longer, so I slip out and close the door.

I find the elevators and push the UP button. I need to be out of here like five minutes ago. But nothing happens, and I wonder whether there's some sort of code I don't know.

I head back out the way I came. I get to the third deck, then rush down to Medical and wave open the door. A woman in scrubs, red-headed and heavy, sits at the desk staring at me like I've got three ears.

"May I help you?" she asks.

"No, thanks. I'm good." I wave at her and rush out the other door, though I know it's stupid. She saw me, and she'll talk when they start asking questions. Maybe even before. But I can't go back and off her now. I just can't. I need to readjust. She can wait.

I take off my glasses and the wig and put them in my pocket. I'll throw them all into the sea tomorrow.

26

A SICK MAN

E mma's pager goes off as she's getting ready for her morning clinic. Two heartbeats later, her phone starts ringing, so she forgets about a shower and bursts out the door in the wrinkled scrubs she slept in without brushing her teeth. But from the chaos swarming Medical, nobody will care.

The whole stretcher team, four stewards in green uniforms, plus two officers in white shirts and three mechanics, by their overalls, stands in the waiting room, bleary-eyed and terrified, and Emma wonders what happened.

She squeezes between them into the ICU, where the whole medical team except Sue works on the man on the stretcher. On a tall table by the bed, Basuki prepares the equipment for intubation while Linda struggles to obtain the patient's vitals. At the head of the bed, Dana squeezes the blue air bag with one hand and holds the mask on his face with the other, trying to ventilate the man's lungs, but the obscene farting noises make it obvious that she doesn't have a good seal.

Emma grabs a pair of gloves and steps closer. With her thumbs on the mask, she curls her fingers around the man's jaw and pulls his face up to get a better seal. The noise stops.

"Thanks, Emma." Dana wipes her forehead on her shoulder.

"What have we got?" Emma asks.

Basuki shrugs.

"A mechanic who didn't show up for his shift this morning. They went to his cabin to check on him and found him in what sounds like a full-blown seizure. It had stopped by the time they got him here, so I thought he's postictal, but there seems to be more than that. I could hardly feel a pulse, and he's not breathing well. That doesn't jibe with a seizure."

"Depends on what caused the seizure," Emma said. "Does he have a history?"

"I haven't checked yet."

Emma would love to, but she can't leave them right now. She glances at the uniformed officer standing in the door. He's tall, blond, and leads the stretcher team, even though he looks no older than twelve.

"Send someone to find the third nurse, please. And what's this man's name?"

"Singh. Rajiv Singh."

Emma nods. "Can you go to the crew doctor's office and find his chart?"

The officer disappears, and Emma turns to the body on the stretcher. His eyes are closed, and when she gently pries them open, she finds pinpoint pupils. Opioids maybe? Thick arms blue with tattoos came out of his once white cut-off T-shirt, now covered in emesis, and Emma doesn't need to check his shorts to know he's been incontinent. She can tell by the smell. But there's another smell, something that doesn't belong here, and she's not sure what.

"Blood pressure 58/30. Heart rate 35," Linda says, and drops the pressure cuff to work on an IV.

Basuki's eyes turn to Emma.

"I'm afraid to intubate him with this blood pressure. It's so low I think he may arrest."

"I am too, but we don't have a choice. We need to secure the airway, since he's not breathing on his own. I wonder if he aspirated."

"I got an 18 in the right AC," Linda says, spitting out the needle protector. "You want bloods first?"

"We have no time. He needs fluids now, or the bloods won't matter. Hang a bag of fluids under pressure, and if you can get a second IV, that would be even better."

"I'm ready," Basuki says, and Emma steps aside to make room.

Her eyes wild, her hair a mess, Sue bursts into the room.

"What the heck..."

"Can you get an amp of epi and give it IM, please? I wonder if this might be some sort of allergic reaction. And push another amp into a bag to make a drip."

Sue disappears and the young officer returns with the chart.

"Thank you," Emma says.

"I'm in," Basuki says. "The airway was full of emesis. There's no doubt he aspirated."

"I bet. But here's the question: Is he sick because he aspirated, or did he aspirate because he was sick? My bet is on the latter."

Emma opens the chart.

"No history of seizures. No allergies. No meds."

She hands the chart to Basuki and leans to examine the patient. There's no evidence of injury, but he's wheezing up a storm. No wonder, if he aspirated the contents of his stomach.

"Let's give him some nebs. And some decadron."

"One amp of epi IM, correct?" Sue asks.

"Yes, please."

Sue stabs the needle into his deltoid and pushes the plunger in. She leaves to prepare the drip while Emma checks the pulse in his neck. Weak and slow. The epi should kick in at any moment. But that smell…

"Do you guys sense this smell?"

"I do, and I'd rather that I didn't," Dana says, glancing at the soiled shorts.

"No, not that. Something …fruity?"

"I wish," Dana says.

"Second IV in. You want another bag of fluid?" Linda asks.

"Yes, please. We'll piggyback the epi drip into it."

The man shudders, then convulses. His arms and legs contract so hard Emma fears they'll lose the IVs. It's a seizure, so bad the bed clanks against the wall.

"Darn. Let's give him four milligrams of Ativan IV and have another four ready," Emma orders.

"Four?" Sue asks.

"Yep. We have no time to fool around. Whatever this is, it's terrible," Emma says, holding on to the man who flops on the bed like a live fish.

"What do you think this is?"

"If I had to guess, I'd think it's some sort of exposure," Emma says. "Toxicology has never been my strong suit, but he looks cholinergic to me. Remember the SLUDGE syndrome? Salivation, lacrimation, urination, diarrhea, GI upset, and emesis?"

"But from what? There are no insecticides here."

"I bet there are. But there are plenty other things besides insecticides that can do it."

The man seems to settle for a moment, then starts thrashing again.

"Give him another four of Ativan," Emma says.

Sue pushes the medicine in, but nothing changes. The man keeps thrashing, then stops as the monitor goes flat.

That's when Emma finally figures out what she smelled.

Green apple. The man smells like green apple.

27

THE CAPTAIN, AGAIN

As she's heading up to the navigation deck at Captain Van Huis's special invitation, Emma wonders what will happen to her morning clinic. They'll cancel it probably, since the whole medical office is a bloody mess. It will take hours to clean, even after they remove the body. With luck, she'll get to shower and brush her teeth before the evening clinic, which is likely to be a disaster.

She knocks at the open door and the captain nods her in.

"Close the door, please."

She does, then drops into her usual chair without waiting for an invitation. The captain glares at her, and she smiles. He turns his eyes to his papers, as usual, and Emma gets ready for a nap. She never understood what this long silence is for. Is it to allow him to gather his thoughts, or to have her shaking in her boots? If so, her mother could give Captain Van Huis a few lessons.

She crosses her arms and closes her eyes, breathing slow, regular breaths. She's not asleep, just forcing her mind to relax. For some reason, her brain works better when she pays no attention to it. Walking is best, but any low-stakes physical activity helps, as long as she lets it do its job.

"Dr. Steele?"

She opens her eyes.

"Have you fallen asleep?"

Emma shakes her head.

"Not yet."

"Tell me."

"A mechanic was found in his bed, actively seizing. They brought him to Medical still unconscious, hypotensive, and bradycardic. We did everything we could to support his breathing and prevent impending cardiovascular collapse, but he started seizing again. Then he arrested and no matter what we did, we could not get him back."

"I know that."

Emma sighs, wishing for the thousandth time she'd stayed home in New York.

"Why?" the captain asks.

"I don't know. He has no medical history that we know of, and he did not appear to be injured. The blood tests might help us — they were still spinning when I left. But I'm not too optimistic. Our capabilities are limited, so we're unlikely to get more than the regular drug screen, and even that is qualitative only."

"What are you looking for?"

"I'm thinking about exposure. His symptoms were consistent with some sort of cholinergic poisoning."

"You think you could elaborate?"

"The constellation of symptoms he presented with makes me suspect exposure to a substance that affects the acetylcholine receptors present in the brain, the spinal cord, and the neuromuscular junction. Acetylcholine activates these receptors, but overflowing them causes their functional paralysis. Nicotine toxicity classically manifests in a biphasic pattern: an initial activation followed by marked inhibition, resulting in paralysis, cardiovascular collapse, and death."

"Thank you. I wish I hadn't asked. So, what sort of substance are you talking about?"

"Insecticides. Certain medications. Some plants. Certain nerve agents. And nicotine."

"Nicotine?"

"Yes. Concentrated nicotine, like that in e-vapes, can be very toxic. In high concentration, it can kill."

The captain sighs.

"I knew I could rely on you to find some far-fetched explanation for what I hope is just a natural death."

"I hope so too, Captain."

"How can you confirm if your suspicion is correct?"

"We took samples of blood, urine, stool, and gastric contents. A toxicology lab worth its salt should be able to determine if there's anything in abnormal amounts."

"You realize we don't have that on board, don't you?"

"I do, Captain. Do you realize it, when you ask me all these questions before I had time to think about it, let alone research it?"

The captain's eyes widen in surprise.

"I guess you're right. But I'm so used to you always having some cockamamie explanation that I forget."

Emma sighs.

"How about you tell me what I don't know?" she asks.

"His name is Rajiv Singh, and he's been with the company for three years. This is his first contract on the *Sea Horse*. He came to join his buddy Jacopo. By the way, Jacopo is the guy we found dead in the storage room."

"The cyanide guy."

"We don't know that. But could this also be cyanide?"

"No."

"Are you sure?"

"Positive."

"Why not?"

"Because the symptoms don't match."

"So you're saying that these two roommates got poisoned by two different people with two different agents three days apart?"

"I didn't say that."

"What did you say?"

"That I suspected cyanide in the first case, but I'm reasonably sure it's not in this one. And I never said there were two people. Most likely there's just one. How many killers can one have on one ship?"

"You tell me, Dr. Steele. You have a knack for stumbling over them. Is this your fourth?"

"Third. I don't think there's more than one killer."

"But why would they change their modus operandi, then? That cyanide, if that's what that was, served them well. Why would they move to something else?"

"Because they had to? Cyanide is extremely dangerous, especially in closed spaces. Maybe he dared to use it in that massive warehouse, but he worried he'd drop dead in a tiny cabin?"

The captain sighs.

"This is all just supposition. The deaths can be unrelated and random. By the way, this guy had typed a message on his phone, asking for forgiveness, but never sent it. This could be a suicide. That could explain why that happened inside his cabin. He wanted privacy."

Emma shrugs, unconvinced.

"Thank you, Dr. Steele. Keep an eye out and let me know if any other exciting ideas cross that mind of yours."

28

A RELUCTANT SEDUCTRESS

Leila stares in the mirror, trying to recognize the woman looking back. Her blonde hair, usually loose or in a messy ponytail, is flattened within an inch of its life. It looks gold-plated as it frames her face. The smoky makeup and the heavy mascara make her blue eyes look huge. But what's most shocking are her lips, blood-red and glossy, thanks to the new lipstick Selim bought her.

The low-cut red dress hugs her tight and ends way above the knee, making her feel self-conscious. She keeps pulling it down, but it climbs back up with every step, uncovering her legs to up there. Other than the flat sandals, she looks like a harlot. She drew the line at neck-breaking high heels.

There's a soft knock at the door. Leila glances at Ayisha. Curled on her side in her pink pajamas, with her thumb in her mouth, she's fast asleep and shows no sign of waking up.

Leila opens the door. Selim steps in, studies her from head to toe, and whistles.

"Wow! You look smashing! I've never seen you look like this," he says, trying to grope her breast. Leila slaps his hand aside.

"And you're unlikely to ever see me again. I look cheap and pathetic."

"Are you kidding? You look beautiful, sexy, and mysterious. Better than I even hoped for. Are you ready?"

"No, I'm not. Does it matter?"

"Probably not. Let's go through it once more. You go up to the ninth deck to the stern, to the Ocean Bar."

"Yes."

"You scan the room. He should be there, at the little table behind the piano in the corner. That's where he is most evenings at nine, listening to the music and having his drink. There's his picture."

"I've seen it plenty, thanks."

"What's his name?"

"Jan."

"So what do you do?"

"I enter the bar like I'm looking for someone. If he's not there, I sit at the bar and order a drink."

"Where do you sit?"

"Facing both doors, so I can see him come in."

"Good. And if he's there?"

"I go to his table and ask if he's Paul."

"And?"

"If he says no, I act angry that the guy stiffed me. We hooked up on Tinder, but he didn't come. I ask if I can sit with him."

"Excellent. Then you order two drinks."

"What if he says no?"

"What?"

"What if he doesn't want me at his table?"

"Are you kidding? Did you look in the mirror? He won't."

"What if he's with someone? Or what if he's not into girls?"

"You think I didn't research him every way from Sunday?

He'll be there, and he's into girls. But if anything doesn't happen as planned, you just come back. That's all there is to it. We'll come up with another plan. But for now, let's just say that everything works as planned, and you sit with him. Then what?"

"I drop the stuff in his drink and make sure he drinks it. Then I follow him to his cabin and find his ID, his phone, and his laptop and bring them here."

"Excellent. This should take less than an hour. That gives me time to do my thing, then drop everything back in his cabin before he wakes up. We should be all done before midnight."

"If Ayisha wakes up…"

"She won't. Didn't you say she never does?"

"If she does…"

"I'll take care of her. Go."

Leila grabs her bag. The black leather bag is much too big for what she's wearing, but she needs room to put all that stuff in it when she gets it. If she gets it. She's sick to her stomach with worry and has trouble swallowing around the knot in her throat. She never picked up a man in her life. Hopefully, never again.

She opens the door to the Ocean Bar, looking for the table in the corner. It's empty, so she takes a seat at the massive horseshoe-shaped bar that lets her see both doors.

"What can I get you?" a smiling waiter asks.

Leila looks at the shelves.

"I'll have a white wine, please."

"A Chardonnay? A Viognier?"

"Chardonnay."

She sits and sips on the wine, keeping an eye on the doors and listening to the music. The pianist, a brown man in his thirties, is so gaunt she wonders if he's sick, but his delightful music helps her relax. She wonders how long she should wait, when a man stops by her side.

"May I sit?" he asks.

He's tall, handsome, and gray-haired. He smiles an admiring smile as he takes her in from head to toe. Leila wonders what to do. But there's nothing she can do but let him sit, though she needs company like she needs a hole in the head. Her mouth is so dry she drains her glass.

"May I buy you another?" he asks.

"No, thanks." Leila stands to leave just as her prey steps in. His thin blonde hair hangs limp around a wide face untouched by the sun, with wire glasses sitting on a bulbous nose and a fleshy chin. He's not handsome, but doesn't look unkind. Her heart racing, Leila follows him to his table. His eyes round in surprise, and Leila forgets what she's supposed to do.

"May I sit with you, please? I'm... trying to escape a man at the bar."

"Sure," he says, looking at the bar. "Is there a problem?"

"No, I'm just not into getting picked up in bars," Leila says, and her cheeks catch fire as his eyes slide from her blood-red lips to her cleavage, then lower. She can almost hear him think: *Then you shouldn't dress like a harlot.* But he looks away and signals to a waiter.

"Can I buy you a drink, then?"

"Yes, please."

"What would you like?"

"Whatever you're having."

He shrugs. "Two dry Hendricks martinis with a twist and three olives."

The waiter leaves, and he turns to her.

"I'm Jan."

"Leila."

"How are you enjoying the cruise, Leila?"

"Quite a bit. I'm looking forward to Egypt. You?"

"Egypt is interesting. But I can't wait to get to Petra. I've heard it's stupendous, but I've never seen it. I promised myself that this time I'll take the day off."

"A day off? From what?"

"I work on the ship."

"Really? What do you do?"

"Just administrative stuff." The waiter brings their drinks and sets them on the table with a bowl of warm nuts.

"Cheers," Jan says, lifting his glass.

"Cheers," she answers, steadying her hand to not spill her drink.

"You enjoy working on the ship?" she asks, while wondering how on earth she can drop the stuff in his drink without him noticing.

"Sometimes more than others."

"Hey, Jan!"

A white-haired woman looking like a model waves to Jan from another table.

"Excuse me for a second."

Leila pulls the pill from her pocket and drops it in his drink, hoping nobody saw her. Seconds later, he's back.

"That's the problem with working on the ship. It's twenty-four seven, and you're never off. Now, what were we talking about?"

"Petra. You were telling me about it."

29

BREAKDOWN

S elim was right. Twenty minutes after finishing his drink, Jan's eyes lose focus and seem to take on a life of their own, looking in opposite directions.

"Are you OK?" Leila asks.

"Yes."

"How about we go to your cabin?"

"How about it?" he says, but doesn't move. Leila helps him up and leads him to the door, hoping nobody's watching.

"Where is your cabin?" she asks, cursing Selim in her mind. She should have asked him.

But even though Jan's brain seems fogged, his body knows where to go. He takes her down a set of stairs and heads to the bow, which is at the opposite end of the ship, and stops by an unmarked door.

He waves a magnetic key and the door clicks, opening to a narrow corridor with only five doors. He stops at the second one, labeled 8002.

He waves his key again, and the door pops open just as Leila thinks of another unanticipated problem. What if he wants sex? She curses herself for not considering this earlier.

There she is, with a man twice her size she drugged into lust. Now what?

She clutches her bag, ready to hit him if he tries anything, but she need not have worried. He wavers, then drops on the unmade bed and starts snoring.

Leila sighs with relief and looks around. The cabin is cramped, with the double bed by the wall filling most of the room and an ancient TV taking the desk under the window. A bookshelf hangs above a ratty loveseat that must have seen better days.

She starts a feverish search for whatever Selim might find useful. She grabs the key he dropped on the desk and puts it in her bag, then empties his pockets and takes everything but the coins. There's a laptop on a charger and an iPad on another. She takes them both, as well as his two cellphones and the clunky ship phone she found in his pocket. She leaves the pager but grabs the folder in the drawer with whatever's in it. She has no time to check.

She glances through the bathroom just in case. Nothing. She's ready to leave when someone knocks on the door.

Leila freezes. There's no place to hide in this six-by-six feet cabin. All she can do is hope they can't come in. But what if they have a key? They needed one to get through the unmarked door that led to the private little hallway.

They knock again.

Her heart racing, Leila drops on the bed next to him and pulls the covers all the way to their necks. She covers her face with her arm, and waits, holding her breath.

The lock clicks, and Leila feels the air draft on the back of her neck as the door opens. Someone chuckles and leaves. The door clicks closed, and Leila gets up, swimming in sweat. She'll never ever forget this. She glances through the cabin once more; then, her heart racing, she opens the door. Nobody.

She heads out the way she came, trying to act like she belongs here but knowing she doesn't. She's never been so terrified, not even when her parents threw her out of the house. But, thank God, she's done.

She opens the door to her cabin to find Ayisha and Selim asleep on the bed without a worry in the world, and her stomach can't take it anymore. She rushes to the bathroom and retches until she's empty, then rinses her mouth and goes to shake Selim's shoulder.

"There you are." She hands him the bag.

He takes a moment to wake up, then a smile spreads across his face.

"You did it! You did it! I knew you would, my beautiful." He leans to kiss her, but she can't stand his touch. She steps back.

"Don't you have work to do? He'll be up in less than two hours, you said. Better hurry."

"You're right. I love you. I'll be back."

Leila takes a long, hot shower, scrubbing the makeup, the sleaze, and the stress off her skin until she looks and feels like herself.

She lies in bed by Ayisha, caressing her hair and inhaling her clean, child smell she loves so much. "Oh, how I love you, baby girl," she whispers. "You'll never know it, but I'm doing this for you."

Her heart slows down, and she lets herself drift asleep when the door opens.

"I'm done. There. Take them back." Selim throws her the black bag. The shock makes Leila dizzy.

"Are you kidding me? You were supposed to do it."

"I couldn't find the freaking cabin. You go. You've been there; you know where it is."

Leila is so angry she's sick.

"You said…"

"I don't care what I said. I don't give a hoot of what I said, and neither should you. What I'm telling you now is go put this stuff back, or you'll be sorry. You think they don't have you on every camera on the freaking ship? If you don't want them here in the morning, asking you what you did and why, go get rid of this stuff. Now."

"But it's been almost two hours. What if he's awake?"

Selim shrugs.

"The sooner you go, the more likely he is to still be asleep. I'd hurry if I were you."

30

SUEZ CANAL

A red sky to the east shows that the sun is about to come up over the Mediterranean as Emma and Guinness take their morning walk, and they couldn't be more excited.

Guinness lifts her nose to the wind, analyzing the fascinating news coming at her from all directions. She's so eager to learn more that she stands on her hind legs and leans over the banister to sniff better.

What is she smelling? Emma wonders, sad that her nose can't compare. She has only her eyes and ears to learn more about this amazing place. They're crossing through the Suez Canal today, which is narrow enough to let her see both shores, and that's a welcome sight after so many days with nothing but water.

What surprises her most is the difference between the two sides. There's nothing but desert on the left. An endless sea of sand, with rarely a hut.

But there's plenty to see on the right, where square buildings and palm trees give way to small parcels of cultivated land in so many hues the ground looks like a quilt. Patches of dark green and orange make room for the brown of bare earth replaced by more green, this one so light it's almost yellow, and Emma would love to know what they are. Once in a while, tiny houses huddle in a village that sits close to the water.

They are on their third lap around the deck when they hear someone run behind them. Emma shortens Guinness's leash to make room, but the jogger turns out to be Archie. He slows down to join them, much to Guinness's delight, and Emma wishes he wouldn't.

"Go on, please," she says, but Archie shakes his head.

"Are you kidding? I looked for an excuse to stop. No way. Isn't this amazing?"

"It certainly is."

"Such a remarkable construction. The Suez Canal is only 120 miles long and 500 feet wide, but by joining the Mediterranean with the Red Sea, it shortens the journey between Europe and Asia by weeks. It's the fastest way between the Atlantic and the Indian Ocean, so more than a hundred ships cross it every day. Do you remember a few years ago when that large container ship, the Ever Given, got knocked off course by the wind and got stuck across the canal, blocking the navigation? That was an international disaster. By the time they got it back to business, the price of oil had already risen."

"Why?"

"Because the canal carries more than half of all the oil transported by sea, plus a substantial percentage of the natural gas. Closing the Suez Canal throttled the whole world's energy supply. Many ships, especially those loaded with perishable items like cattle and fruit, couldn't afford to wait, so they took the route around Africa through the Cape of Good Hope. That took weeks, and it required tons of extra oil, increasing the oil demand."

"I find it amazing that the two sides are so different. What countries are they in?"

"Egypt."

"Both?"

"Yep. The Suez Canal separates most of Egypt from the Sinai Peninsula, but that also belongs to Egypt. The canal is one of Egypt's most important sources of foreign currency. To cross it one way, a container ship must pay almost a million dollars, so just think what that must mean for Egypt's treasury. But it looks like they are running out of luck.

"Why?"

"Haven't you heard the news?"

"Nope. I don't watch the news. It's always about war, crime, pandemics, corruption, or some other sort of misery, and I see plenty of that on the job. But what's the news?"

"Hamas made a raid into Israel, killed thousands of people and took hundreds of prisoners into Gaza. Israel's troops entered Gaza to get them, and they're crushing it bit by bit. As if all that wasn't bad enough, the Yemeni-based Houthi rebels attacked a couple of ships in the Red Sea to force the world to pay attention to what's happening in Gaza and force Israel to stop their operations. The whole place is on fire, so a bunch of shipping companies have already rerouted their ships, trying to avoid the Red Sea. Yesterday, even our captain wasn't sure whether we will continue on our scheduled itinerary through the Suez Canal to the Red Sea or would be told to turn around in the Mediterranean and get rerouted. But they apparently decided to go ahead and move the ship to Asia for the winter, rather than reschedule every cruise for the coming six months, which would be a financial disaster. They are betting we'll make it through. In six months, the conflict should be over and it will be safe to return. I hope they are right."

"Me too."

"On a happier note, what will you do in Petra?"

"Work, probably. I don't think I'll get the day off."

"If you do, keep in mind there's a two-hour drive from the port to the excavations, so it's a whole day affair."

"Oh well. That puts it out of my reach. I might watch your lecture and look at pictures."

"If you don't, I have a great video to show you. It's not quite the same thing as being there, but you'll get the gist of it."

"That would be nice."

They walk together in pleasant companionship, and Emma wonders if she misjudged him the first time they met, or she's misjudging him now. He seems polite, informed, and even funny. But that doesn't mean he can't also be many less pleasant things too.

Guinness finds something fascinating and tries to squeeze under a low bench. Emma pulls her back, worried she'll eat something she shouldn't, when her pager goes off. Two seconds later, her phone rings just as the Bright Star signal bursts out of the speakers.

"Bright Star at deck seven, stern. Bright Star at deck seven, stern."

Emma stares at Guinness, wondering what to do. She can't take her to a code, but she has no time to take her back to Hanna's cabin.

"I'll take her back so you can go," Archie says. Emma hands him the leash and runs.

31

SUE

Emma follows the two stretcher team members running up the crew stairs. The men step aside to let her pass, and Emma wishes they didn't. She does her best to keep up the pace, but by the time she reaches deck seven, her heart wants to burst out of her chest and she's ready to heave. I really need to work out more, she tells herself, turning toward the stern. At the end of the hallway, she pushes the heavy door that closes the hallway, then another, this one watertight, going outside.

The small outdoor space is packed with uniforms. Emma squeezes between them to find the patient, but she's late. Kneeling on the metal deck, a sweaty steward is performing chest compressions. Another awaits his turn behind the medical team gathered around the body, looking grim.

Linda works on IV access. Kneeling by the patient's head, Dana squeezes the blue bag with shaky hands while Basuki holds the mask.

The man performing CPR moves aside to make room for another, and Emma catches a glimpse of the body. It's a woman, fair-skinned and generously built, and she's naked. The wet hair plastered to her head and the puddle of water around her make it clear she was found in the water.

The tiny outdoor space on deck seven is nicknamed the lover's heaven for a reason. It's hard to access, sheltered from prying eyes, and only big enough for a hot tub. Renting it is not cheap, and guests must reserve it ahead, but then they have it to themselves for the hour or two they booked it for, and it comes with champagne, chocolate, and roses. That's why they call it the Honeymoon Balcony, though those who book it are rarely honeymooners.

"What have we got?" Emma asks.

"They found her in the whirlpool when they came to clean it in the morning," Basuki says. "That's all we know. We gave her two rounds of epi with no ROSC. I think she's been dead for a while, but the hot water kept her warm."

Emma sighs and kneels by the head. She brushes the wet strands of hair from her face and pries open the eyes. The pupils are fixed, dilated, and unreactive to light.

"You're right. Let's do one more round of epi and call it if nothing happens. It would be a pity to bring back a body without a brain."

Basuki gives her a strange look, but says nothing. The man doing CPR steps aside to make room for another.

"Third epi given," Linda says, her voice flat.

"How long have you guys been doing this?" Emma asks.

"Nineteen minutes now."

Emma studies the body. The heavy breasts flop around with each chest compression like fish trying to escape, and the rounded belly jiggles, but the legs are long and shapely. She wasn't old, Emma thinks. Forties, maybe? My age.

She checks her watch. Time to call the code.

"Thank you all for your outstanding work. Unfortunately,

our patient failed to respond. We'll call the time of death at 6:48."

The man performing CPR joins his colleagues. Basuki takes the mask off the face, and Emma brushes the strands of wet hair off the cheeks so white they look blue.

That's when she recognizes Sue.

32

NO WAY OUT

Emma's eyes burn and her heart is heavy as lead as she returns to her cabin after this dreadful day. It started with finding Sue, then continued with the mandatory meeting with the captain and two atrocious clinics that lasted most of the day. This evening she's worn out, defeated, and feels like this is all her fault.

That's not new. She's always felt guilty for everything; Mother dear saw to that. It was always Emma's fault, from any grade that was less than perfect to Mother's foul moods that were more frequent than her changing socks. Emma was expected to always apologize for everything. That's why even today, she still apologizes when some oblivious person bumps into her. Her "I'm sorry" comes out before she can think, and boy, does that make her angry! But this time it's different. She should have been able to untangle these threads and make sense of these deaths, but she failed. And, as expected, the chat with the captain was no fun.

"What happened?" he asked.

"The lead nurse was found dead in the honeymooners' whirlpool."

"I know that."

"Well, then. Why don't you tell me what you know?" Emma snapped, sitting on her hands to refrain from throwing something at him. "It was all over by the time I got there."

The captain gave her a strange look, but, for once, he answered her question.

"The whirlpool was not booked for last night. She must have gotten in with her passkey. They found an empty bottle of champagne and one glass. That's all I've got. What do you have?"

"Not much. It looked like a drowning. She had water in her airway, and I saw no injuries or any signs of violence. We drew blood and urine, but the labs are still spinning."

"That's it?"

"For now."

"So you think she got so drunk that she drowned in the whirlpool?"

"I doubt that, though it's a possibility."

"Dr. Steele, do you realize this is the third death we have had on this ship since we left Istanbul a week ago?"

"I do."

"So you think all these deaths are accidental?"

Upon hearing his manufactured outrage, Emma couldn't help but laugh. For a week now, she's been trying to get him to acknowledge the danger, and now he blames her for not being wary enough. That's ironic, but still better than telling her there's nothing to worry about.

"No, Captain, I do not think her death is accidental. That is why I collected evidence for a rape kit, even though I think it's most unlikely to find anything after she sat in that tub for hours. Supposing there was something to find."

"A rape kit?"

"Yes. I collected samples from her vagina, her mouth, and

her anus, as well as hair samples and such. We also gathered her clothes in a bag. Wouldn't you like to know if she had sex before she died?"

"I guess I would. When will you have the results?"

"Only after we send them to a specialized lab. That's not something we can do on the ship, but I thought it might provide us with important information. Who knows? We may even get some DNA, though I seriously doubt it."

As she left, the captain told her that Dana was going to operate as the Medical's lead until the Aurora company sent them a new nurse. Then Emma went straight into her clinic, which was a zoo. The rumor that something exciting had happened that had to do with Medical had spread like wildfire, so every busybody came to learn more, as if anyone would tell them anything.

When the evening clinic was finally over, Emma went to her cabin and pulled out the bottle of Johnny Walker she had hidden in her closet for days such as this.

She hadn't liked Sue one bit. The woman had been a bitch since the first day they met, and she never stopped. But having someone from her team, even someone as obnoxious as Sue, die like that, made her weary. Emma doesn't understand what's going on, but she knows that this ship is cursed. For some reason, evil chose to embark on this ship, so nobody on it is safe. That's why she's worried about Dana, Linda, and Basuki. Hanna too.

But there's nobody she's more worried about than Guinness. All the others chose to be here, but Guinness is here because of Emma. She should send her home. But how?

The easiest thing would be to take her home herself. She's not in jail, after all. Sure, she has a work contract, but people leave their jobs all the time. They won't tie her to the freaking desk if she chooses to leave. All she needs to do is grab her passport and the dog, buy a plane ticket, and go home. Their next port, the day after tomorrow, is Aquaba, in Jordan. That's the departure for Petra. She could disembark in Aquaba, take a taxi to Amman, then get on a flight to New York. She could have Guinness home in three days.

She gets so excited about the idea of leaving the ship she forgets to drink her whisky as she looks for flights.

But there's a problem. First, she has to recover her passport that the Human Resources office holds under lock and key. The company doesn't want their crew members to just pack and leave whenever they feel like it, so they may give her trouble.

Second, she's not sure what would happen to Guinness. Will they want to quarantine her? She has all her vaccination certificates, of course, but what if that's not enough for the Omani authorities?

And third, she's not exactly proud to abandon her team, especially now that they're already one person down. If she leaves, they'll go from five to three overnight, and still have to care for almost five thousand souls. The Aurora company will certainly send someone to replace her, but that may take a while.

I can't do that, she thinks. *No matter how much I hate the ship, and the senseless rules, and the fact that I can't fix this disaster, I can't run away. One way or another, I have to see it through. Once we reach Dubai, I'll go home.*

Her phone rings just as she opens the whisky. She glances at the pager, but it's quiet, so it's probably not Medical.

"Yes?"

"Emma?"

"Hanna?"

"Can you come by? Guinness doesn't look good."

33

READY TO GO

I'm watching the news, and seeing how awful things are in Gaza gets me gutted. Gaza city got blown into rubble, and thousands of people, many of them women and children, got killed. More are likely to follow, so the survivors are fleeing south to escape the carnage. The roads are clogged with cars, bicycles, and donkeys overburdened with people's life possessions: carpets, pots, plastic bags full of stuff. Men pushing overloaded carts carry buckets and children. Women wail for the dead. Palestine's future looks bleak.

That makes my mission so much more essential. There was no inkling of this five years ago, when I was just one of the many idealistic students of Palestinian descent at NYU, studying for my college degree and looking to change the world.

When one of my upperclassmen talked to me about joining our brothers' cause and bringing the fight back to the Jews, I jumped at it. I forgot I was American, and I was ready to go all in, but he said I wasn't ready.

"Listen, Selim, you are a kind man and a good Muslim.

You're smart as a whip, big-hearted, and have lots of potential, but there's a long way to go before you can be a real asset to the movement. We don't need more cannon fodder; we have plenty of that. We need thinkers and leaders and skilled men who can execute our most daring plans. With your American passport, good looks, and education, you could get far, but you'll first have to put in the work. Any twelve-year-old shepherd can blow himself up to kill a few Jews, but that's not how we will win this war and liberate our people. You need to be ruthless, patient, and cunning, and you need a team."

That's why I stayed with my studies, and I looked for a partner. Leila was perfect — beautiful, smart, and all alone. She had no family or friends I needed to worry about finding out my secret. Nobody but the kid, which was a problem, but also an opportunity. Through her, I found my way to Leila's heart. The sex helped, but it only came later.

Two years later, my friends told me to apply for an internship at the Fincantieri S.p.A., in Genoa, one of the world's greatest shipbuilders.

"Learn everything about that ship," they said, "until you can find your way around it with your eyes closed. Find out how every little thing on it works, how to fix it, and how to break it."

That ship was the *Sea Horse*.

At the time, I didn't understand how that could help Palestine, but I did it anyway. I applied myself to it as if my life depended on it, and six months later, I finished my internship with a boring but profound knowledge of cruise ships in general and the *Sea Horse's* unique systems in particular. From a drunk IT specialist who wanted to bed me, I got the ship's login credentials for remote maintenance. Even better, I managed to steal them without having to get horizontal.

Now, after years of hard work, I'm finally within sight of my goal. A few more days, and I'll get to use what I learned to benefit my people, even though things didn't go as smoothly as I hoped. Not with Jacopo — that one, I knew from the beginning I would have to off. I couldn't afford to spare someone who could thwart my plans with a few careless words. But I wish that other guy had minded his own business. Getting rid of him was no fun, and, even worse, exposed me to that nurse.

I agonized about her for a day. Would she recognize me without the wig and the glasses? Probably not, but I had to make sure.

So last night I pretended to bump into her by mistake. I apologized and introduced myself; then I bought her a drink, and one thing led to another. We were kissing in the whirlpool when she said, "You know, something about you feels oddly familiar. I feel like I've met you before."

"Don't I wish!" I poured her another glass of champagne and added in the GHB.

Twenty minutes later, her eyes lost focus. She didn't even put up a fight when I held her face under water. I watched her blink in surprise as the bubbles coming out of her mouth mixed with those of the hot tub. So strange how they were all the same, whether they came from a machine or carried someone's soul. I couldn't tell them apart.

I left her fingerprints on the bottle and threw my glass overboard, then got out and wiped myself, making sure I didn't leave a wet trail behind. I was drained by the time I made it to my cabin. That's why I'm watching the news: to remind myself why I'm doing this and gather strength. There's power in anger. But now, after seeing my people's suffering, I feel re-energized. I turn off the TV to review the plans when my phone rings.

"Yes."

"Where have you been?"

Leila. What the heck got into her? Ever since we got on this ship, she's been a bitch. For years, she'd been sweet and obedient. She always did exactly what I told her. But now, no matter what I need her to do, she has a problem. That night I sent her back to the engineer's cabin, she blew a gasket. I had to slap her to bring her to her senses. And now she harasses me again.

"I've been out, working. What do you need?"

"I've tried the password. It doesn't work."

"What do you mean, it doesn't work?"

"Just as I said. I tried it twice, and it won't let me in. I'm afraid to try again for fear I'll set off an alarm. How long ago did you get this password?"

I try to remember.

"Ten months? One year?"

"They must have changed it since then."

My blood turns to ice. It never crossed my mind they'd change the password, though it should have. The people at the shipyard do the regular maintenance and software updates remotely. I should have realized they would change the passwords for safety.

"What do we do now?" Leila asks.

"I have no choice but to break into the systems room. Unfortunately, that's always manned with at least two people. From there, there's no turning back."

But there's no turning back anyhow.

34

THE BOX

As I hang up, my mouth's so full of bile I could puke. Part of me wants to blame Leila, hoping she made a mistake, but deep inside, I know better. She's a better hacker than I am. That's the main reason I brought her, though her being a good-looking female didn't hurt. She might not have the same drive as I do, but if she says the password doesn't work, the password doesn't work. Trying again will only get us in trouble. Like it or not, it's time for the box, though it's earlier than I had planned. I don't want any of that stuff in my cabin — or in Leila's, for that matter — so that some stupid steward stumbles over it when he cleans the room. That's just what happened to the team that hijacked the *Achille Lauro*, forcing them to act when they weren't yet ready. But I have no choice. I need to break into the systems control room, and that's the most secure place on the ship, more so than the freaking navigation deck. There are never less than two people there, usually three, to ensure nothing suspicious endangers the ship. I had hoped to do it remotely, but that didn't work.

I put on my dark hoodie, wishing I still had the wig and

the glasses, but I panicked and threw them overboard after that nurse saw me. I close the door softly and head down to deck two, where my box ought to be.

But what if it's not?

A cold shiver goes down my spine, and my mouth turns dry. If that box is gone, it's all over. There's no way can I overpower this whole damn ship without my equipment. If the box is gone, all I can do is take Leila and the kid ashore in Aqaba and never come back. I can only hope that nobody wonders where we've gone and why, or makes any connection with the three murders. But that's highly unlikely. That box better be there.

I tiptoe down the stairs like a cat ready to leap, but fortunately, nothing happens. It's late enough that the hallways are all empty, thank Allah. Things are going right, for once. I get to deck three, where my legal trail is over. I can pass through Medical as I did before, or I can brave the massive door marked "CREW ONLY," go straight, and hope that nothing happens. But, since the shortest way between two points is not the straight one but the one you know, I open the door to Medical again. After all, how many times can I be that unlucky? It's past midnight. They must all be asleep.

This is my lucky day. The door to Medical clicks open, and I'm in and out in two breaths. I'm back in the in the gray hallway I know, and my heart slows down a little.

I walk past the row of office doors, hoping that nobody's working late, and find the stairs. I step down as silent as a ghost, then head to my box that's calling me.

The vast storage room is darker than the insides of a shark. I pull out my flashlight and zigzag between the shelves to the corner. There she is, my beauty, but they've covered her in crap. Boxes of toner and printer paper and God knows what else. What the heck? Couldn't they put them some-where else, I wonder, as I hold the flashlight between my teeth and pile the crap to the side to open the lid. It doesn't take long, but that's a job I could have done without. I dial the code to open the box.

I'm so shaky it takes me three tries to dial my mother's birth date. The lid springs open.

I pull out the bubble-wrapped gypsum Aphrodite I stuck in there, worried that the jerk would look inside. Fortunately, it's hollow, so it's light.

I set it aside and try to decide what I need the most. I can't take everything, since I have no room. I'll come back for the rest when I need it.

I choose two grenades and lay them gently in my backpack. They are the last thing I hope to need, but they'll come in handy if I get outnumbered. At least I'll go out with a bang. I add three cans of pepper spray, the white plastic canister of nerve gas, and the green one with sleeping gas, which is bigger. I don't know how I'll break into the systems room yet, so I need to leave my options open. I take the Glock and the respirator, which I will need if I end up gassing a room.

I'd love to take the AR-15, but it wouldn't fit in my backpack. I tell myself I'll take it next time, then, almost as an afterthought, I grab the stunner. Not sure what I'll use it for, but it can't hurt to have a silent way to disable uninvited visitors.

I pick up Aphrodite to put her back into her box when bright light floods the room. A choked voice speaks behind me.

"Drop that. Drop that right away and put your hands on your head."

I breathe with relief. The worst has finally happened, so I don't have to worry about it anymore. I only have to deal with it. I lay down Aphrodite in her bubble-wrap gown and pick up the stunner.

"Turn around with your hands on your head."

"But I did nothing wrong," I say, like every criminal in history, just to get his brain muddled. I pivot on my left foot and aim the stunner at him.

"Drop that," he says. "Drop it now."

"Sure, officer. I'll do that right now," I say, to scramble his frightened brains even further. That kid's not an officer; he's just one of the underpaid security guys who knows nothing more than how to check passengers' IDs and make sure they bring no booze on the ship, so the company can make more money. He's shaking so hard I bet he never shot anyone. It would be a wonder if he remembers how to release the safety.

He stares at me with wide-open eyes as I aim the stunner at his neck. I pull the trigger and watch him drop the gun and crumble.

I'm sorry for the guy, but he chose to get in the way. *That was a bad idea and not my fault,* I think, giving his head a quick twist until I hear the crack.

It's even easier than they taught me in training. There, we fought, and I was just as likely to get hurt as I was to subdue them. Often more so. But this poor guy was out of his league.

Now what?

I have a dead guard, a backpack full of weapons, a box which is still mostly full, and a cheap statue of Aphrodite. Isn't life interesting?

I undress Aphrodite from her bubble gown and wrap it around the guard. It takes all my strength to lift him and put him in the box, but I manage. It's not ideal, but it will have to do.

I pick up the statue. Thank Allah, this one is light. I lift it on my shoulder and head back to my cabin, knowing that this is complete madness. Nobody could even glance at the security cameras without noticing I carry a statue, but it's better than carrying a corpse.

Once in my cabin, I stand Aphrodite by the door.

"You look after things, will you?" I tell her, and go take a much-needed shower.

This is insane. I'll have to act soon.

35

A SICK PUPPY

E mma rushed up the stairs two at a time. Guinness doesn't look good? How can that be? She was fine this morning. What happened? *What did they do to her,* she thinks, heaving as she drags her doctor's bag up the stairs.

Hanna opens the door before she gets to knock, and Emma bursts in.

Guinness is lying on her side on Hanna's love seat. She looks at Emma and wags her tail, but she doesn't jump to meet her as usual. She doesn't even lift her head, and Emma's heart sinks.

She kneels by the loveseat to pet her, and Guinness submits to the touch. She licks her hand, but she doesn't jump to play, or even bark. She just gazes at Emma with her honey-colored trusting eyes, and Emma's soul hurts. Something is wrong with her girl, and she doesn't know what. And, even though she's not unfamiliar with nonverbal patients, Emma is not a vet.

"What happened?" she asks.

"She looked fine this morning when Archie brought her

back from her walk. But she wouldn't eat her food. She lapped some water, then lay there for hours doing nothing. That's just not like her."

"No, it's not. Any vomiting? Any diarrhea?"

"No, and no. She was panting and heaving, so I thought maybe she was too hot. I lowered the AC until I had to put on a sweater, but that didn't help. She's been lying there for hours, and I didn't know what to do."

Sick with worry, Emma examines Guinness. Her black nose is warm and dry, which is not good. It should be cold and wet, like it is every time she sticks it where it doesn't belong. She opens her mouth to check her gums and tongue. All pink, wet, and normal. Nothing there, except a few licks. Her eyes look good, and so do the ears.

She proceeds to examine Guinness from her head to her toes, just like she would examine a baby, or another nonverbal patient. She listens to her heart and lungs, palpates every inch of her, looking for signs of pain, and does the same with every bone. She ranges the joints, including the tail, and checks her paws with the webs between toes. Nothing.

She flips her on her back. Guinness doesn't protest; she just looks at her with sorrowful eyes that seem to say, "Why did you do this to me? I was a good girl," and Emma's soul shatters.

She rubs her belly, which Guinness usually loves, but now she seems wary. She palpates it gently, while Guinness watches warily. She seems distended, but not too tender.

"What did she eat last night?"

"Her food. She was fine. And I think she stole one of my peaches. She loves peaches."

Hanna averts her eyes, and Emma can bet Guinness stole nothing. Hanna gave it to her and is covering her tracks.

"Did you find the pit?"

"No."

Emma looks under the bed and the tables, in the corners, and everywhere else. Nothing. She turns to Guinness.

"Did you swallow that peach pit?"

Guinness looks away, pretending she doesn't understand. Emma sighs.

She pulls the dog up into a sit, puts her hands around her stomach and squeezes.

"What are you doing?" Hanna asks.

"Getting that pit out."

She squeezes Guinness again and again. The Heimlich maneuver is not meant for dogs, and it's not for a GI obstruction. The Heimlich is meant for people choking on their food, but that's the best Emma has got for the moment, and she needs to do something.

She holds the dog between her legs and presses on her stomach with all her might. Guinness tolerates it politely, like she puts up with all the silly things Emma comes up with, like brushing her teeth and trimming her nails, but she doesn't look happy. Her sharp ears are flat to her head, and her tail between her legs reaches her chin. Still, nothing happens. She growls, warning Emma she's had enough of this foolishness, when all of a sudden, she coughs, then retches out a peach pit that hits the floor and rolls under the bed.

A heartbeat later, she leaps out of Emma's squeeze, licks her nose, and without skipping a beat, devours her uneaten breakfast before one could count to thirty.

"There now. She's feeling better," Hanna says.

Emma leans back, too exhausted to smile.

"Looks like it."

"You, however, look like death warmed over. You must have had a terrible day, with the lead nurse drowning and all. Let me get you a drink."

"How do you know about the lead nurse?"

"My steward told me. She apparently had a taste for young men. There's a debate between those who think she got so drunk that she drowned, and those who think she got offed by the young man she was with."

"What young man?"

"Someone said she had drinks at the casino bar with a young man and they left together. Tall, dark, and blue eyed, he said."

"Who said that?"

"I don't know. I'll have to ask Budi," Hanna says, just as someone knocks at the door.

36

DINNER WITH FRIENDS

Barking ferociously, Guinness jumps on the door, threatening to rip the intruder to shreds. Hanna pushes her aside to let Archie in, and Guinness licks his face to apologize.

"How's she doing?" he asks, scratching the itchy spot behind her right ear.

"Much better. Emma worked her magic and got her to retch a peach pit."

"A peach pit? Where on earth did she find it?"

Hanna shrugs, looking guilty, and Archie lets it go.

"Excellent. You got me worried. Now that we're all good, how about I buy you ladies some dinner?" Archie asks.

"Not me, thanks. I've had quite a day. I'll just take Guinness for a quick walk and go to bed," Emma says.

"Nonsense. You need to eat. You may as well keep us company," Hanna says.

"I can't. Look at me. I've worn the same scrubs since yesterday."

"Then go to take a shower and change while Archie takes Guinness for a walk. Meet you at the Pearl in an hour."

"Good idea. Guinness, wanna go for a walk?" Archie asks.

The dog jumps on the door, Archie grabs her leash, and they're gone before Emma gets to object. That's why, an hour later, she's waiting at the door of the Pearl, dressed in her eternal black dress.

The atmosphere at the Pearl, *Sea Horse's* main dining venue, is nothing like Ambrosia's understated elegance, and that's for good reasons. Unlike the steakhouse, which seats fewer than a hundred a night and always serves the same menu, down here they have almost three thousand hungry mouths to feed. And, other than a few classics like Cesar salad, onion soup, and cheeseburgers, the menu changes every night. The Pearl is not a place for repose, but a feeding facility of industrial proportions; its elegance is only skin deep. The guests are hungry, thirsty, and impatient, and they pull the weary staff in a dozen directions at once. Beyond the ubiquitous smiles, their stress shows.

A waiter takes Emma to a table by the window where Hanna is already seated and hands her a menu. Outside, the sea froths in waves, since they've crossed the Suez Canal into the Red Sea. Emma only saw it while walking Guinness this morning, then the day crashed on her.

"I missed most of the Suez Canal," she says.

Hanna shrugs.

"If you saw a little, you saw it all. I watched it the whole day, and nothing changed. And, to be honest, I'll be glad when we're out of this mess. The news on TV is depressing."

"Isn't it?" Archie says, taking a seat. In a light blue shirt the color of his eyes and dark well-pressed pants, he looks particularly handsome, and Emma wonders why he wastes his time with her and Hanna when there are plenty of attractive women on the ship.

"Sorry I'm late. I was ready to leave when they showed a tanker attacked by drones in the Red Sea. They were able to down most of them, though one started a small fire. This appears to be just the latest incident since the Houthis declared they'll attack any ship with Jewish connections unless they stop the war in Gaza."

"Thank God the *Sea Horse* is registered in Liberia. But let's speak about something more fun. Food, for example. Are you ready to order?" Hanna asks.

Hanna and Archie order, but Emma struggles to make sense of the menu, which seems to include multiple variations on a five-course dinner. *Who has time for a five-course dinner,* she wonders, but the surrounding tables are all full. Unlike her, who can't find enough hours in the day, the passengers have the whole day to fill, and for many, dinner is the highlight of the day. They look forward to being spoiled with attention and choices.

"I'll have the onion soup and the mushroom pasta." Emma leans back and sips on the house wine, a rather harsh red. "Are you guys looking forward to Petra tomorrow?"

"I look forward to the peace and quiet on the ship," Hanna says. "I expect they'll all be gone, so Guinness and I can have the whole place to ourselves."

"You're not going?" Emma asks.

Hanna shakes her head.

"I can't. There are miles to walk from the parking lot to the site. That's too much for me."

"Miles? Really? How does everyone do that?"

"They don't. They have horse-drawn carriages, camels, and donkeys one can hire, but the company recommends against it. The trip is uncomfortable, and the vehicles are uninsured. It's not cheap either."

"I'm sorry."

"Don't be. Guinness and I will have a great time. How about you, Archie? I assume you'll be going?"

"I will, but I won't have much time to myself. I'm

supposed to lecture on the way to keep the passengers entertained, so I'll be moving from one bus to another, telling the folks what they're about to see. But that's what they pay me for."

"So what is this Petra, after all?" Emma asks.

"One of antiquity's most spectacular sites, an entire city carved in rock. Hundreds of buildings have been sculpted in pink sandstone, and they date from the Nabataeans, an Arabic tribe that settled in Jordan more than 2,000 years ago. Their refined culture reflects in their architecture, and, as desert people, they knew how to collect and manage water, so their ingenious complex of channels and dams is still amazing today. For centuries, Petra was unknown to everyone but the Bedouins. It was discovered in 1812, and the excavations started in 1929, almost a century ago, but most of it has yet to be unearthed."

"Sounds fascinating," Emma says.

"It is. You really should come see it."

Emma sighed.

"I don't see how. Medical is already understaffed, and it's not like I can get away for an hour and see it."

37

THE PLAN

It's almost midnight when there's finally a knock at Leila's door. It's the "all is safe" signal, so she glances at Ayisha to make sure she's asleep — she hasn't seen Selim in weeks, so she'll go nuts if she does — and she opens.

He slips in and pulls the door behind him, then scoops her in his arms, and Leila feels like she finally got home. Oh, how she missed him! She barely saw him since they embarked, and, whenever she did, he was in a rush or had some awful task to give her. He acted so cold and remote that she started to doubt he still loved her. But she forgot it all when he called to tell her he was coming. She spent a whole hour getting ready, but it was all worth it for the way he looks at her.

She hugs him closer and she sinks her face into the hollow of his throat to breathe his scent. He smells like after-shave and sweat and him, and she wants him so bad it makes her dizzy.

When she finally lets go, he glances at Ayisha, who is still asleep, and sits on the loveseat by the window. He pats the seat next to him, then puts his arm around her and she snuggles close.

"How are you doing, my love? And how's our baby?"

"She's OK, just tired of being cooped inside all the time. So am I. I'm afraid that my head will explode if I play another game of snakes and ladders."

"I bet. But the good news is that we're almost ready. A couple more days, and we're done."

"Really? I thought we were going to Dubai."

"God willing, this will be over before Dubai."

"How so? Did you get what you needed?"

"Not yet, but I'm close. In a day or two. Will you help me?"

"Of course. I'll do anything for you, my love."

"I knew I could rely on you, sweetheart. We'll have to strand the ship in the Red Sea."

Leila thinks she heard him wrong.

"Strand the ship? This ship?"

"Yes."

She stares at him, trying to understand.

"But you said we'd break into their network to steal some information, then get away. You never talked about sabotaging the ship."

"Same thing. We still have to break into their network to disable the ship, but we need to disable it so our friends can board it."

"Our friends? What friends?"

"The guys I work with. We all subscribe to the holy mission of eliminating the unfaithful and aim to liberate Palestine. We call ourselves Ansar Allah, God's Supporters, but in America we're known as the Houthis."

Leila's heart freezes.

"The Houthi rebels?"

He ignores her.

"We need to have the ship immobilized for an hour or two so the incoming team can board it, overpower the security, and take over."

Leila's brain is so numb she has trouble understanding what he's saying. The one thing she gets is that he lied to her. She loved him and trusted him, and he lied to her.

"In order to disable the ship, we'll need to access the automation control system for the ship's machinery, which is controlled by a network of PLCs, industrial computers called programmable logic controllers. I hoped to access them remotely with the password, but that didn't work, so I will have to physically access the PLC server.

"A bunch of diesel-electric generators power the electric motors suspended in pods below the hull that make up the ship's propulsion system. The speed of the motors controls that of the ship, and is in turn controlled by a VFD, a variable frequency drive. Multiple sensors feed back into the PLCs to protect the system, such as the motors' operating temperature, which must be below 350 degrees Fahrenheit. If it gets any higher, the VFD shuts down the motors to protect the system.

"To stop the ship, I will need to fake the input signal for the temperature, making it look like the motors are overheating. That will alarm the PLCs and the VFD will shut them down."

Leila tries to listen, but she doesn't understand a thing. PLC? VFD? Sensors? The words swirl through her brain, making no sense whatsoever. All she understands is "Stop the ship."

"What happens after you stop the ship?"

"Our friends will board it and take over."

"Take over what?"

"Everything. The engines, the navigation deck, the radio. The whole ship."

"Then what?"

"I'll restart the engines to enable the ship to restart."

"And then?"

"We will sail it to Yemen."

"What for? Ransom?"

"That too. But the people on the ship are more valuable than the ship itself. Even if you don't count the crew, there are like 3000 passengers. Mostly Americans, but also Australians, British, Dutch, French — whatever. Rich people from the most powerful countries in the world. Their governments will do anything to get them back. By taking them hostage, we could not only stop the carnage in Gaza, but even free Palestine."

"And that's the most important thing to you?"

"Of course. What else?"

Leila looks at him like she's never seen him.

"Do you realize that Ayisha and I are on this ship that you plan to hand to your terrorist friends? You dragged us here with your lies and endangered my child, and now you plan to hand us to the Houthis and you're crazy enough to imagine that I will help you?"

38

PLAN CHANGE

I'm totally drained when I get to my cabin. This must have been the hardest night of my life, and it's nobody's fault but my own. What the heck was I thinking when I brought along Leila and the kid? I've always known that my mission wasn't hers, but I thought she loved me and she'd go along with my plans. Boy, was I stupid. I should have realized she'd worry about the kid. But she wasn't worried, she was enraged.

She looked at me like she wanted to rip my heart out. Tears ran down her cheeks, but her eyes burned with fury.

"You want me to put Ayisha into a hostage situation? Hand her to your fanatical so-called friends? You must be completely out of your mind."

She was shouting so loud I had to cover her mouth or she would have woken up the kid, but she slapped my hand away.

"Listen, Leila, my friends will look at us like heroes. Once we hand them the ship with all the hostages, they'll treat you like a queen. You have nothing to worry about."

"Nothing to worry about when a band of armed terrorists

boards the ship my child is on? Have you seen the news? Have you watched any movies? Nobody here will be safe. Not Ayisha, not me, not even you. Whether we get shot by your terrorists or blown up by whatever SWAT team comes to rescue the ship, nobody will be safe. In the best-case scenario, people will die. In the worst, they'll sink the whole freaking ship."

"Listen, my love. You and Ayisha will lock yourself in your cabin, and nobody will touch a hair on your heads. Trust me."

"Trust you? After you lied to me and dragged me into this freaking mess? And even if nothing happened to Ayisha, what will happen to the thousands of people on this ship? How many will die, how many will get hurt, and how many families will have an empty seat at the dinner table and never again see their loved ones? You are completely insane."

That one I didn't see coming. She's not only worried about her kid, but as an American, she can't stomach the idea of handing thousands of her compatriots to what she thinks of as terrorists. I tried to explain to her that we are all men of faith, freedom fighters, and heroes, but she couldn't care less.

She wasn't that keen on breaking into the ship's network even when I told her that it was to steal some industrial secrets and we'd make tons of money. But taking hostage the ship with the people on it? No way.

The best I could get from her was a promise to stay put for now. She was so furious I worried she'd denounce me, so I told her that if she spoke, she'd land in jail for trying to break into the ship's network and for drugging the engineer and stealing his stuff. With her in jail, Ayisha would end up in foster care. That cooled her down, but I don't know for how long. I gave her a sleeping pill and told her we'll talk again tomorrow, but I'm worried she'll turn me in. We'll see. I'd rather not get rid of her, because then I'd have to get rid of the kid too, and I don't have time for all that now. Maybe after some sleep she'll get her wits about her and settle down.

And like that's not bad enough, since I can't rely on her, I need to modify my plan. It's still a bit rough, but it sounds workable, and I'll finesse it as I think it through.

I can access the ECR, the engine control room, with the keycard Leila stole from the engineer, but that room is never empty. They always have at least one officer and one crew member there, sometimes more. I'm afraid I'll have to use the nerve gas, and that means I'll have to use the respirator. How the heck do I get there with the mask? I don't know. I'll think about it later.

To access the system, I need the notebook computer that I had at Fincantieri to plug into the PLC network. It still has the access credentials we used during my internship, so it should let me enter programming mode. That way I hope to find the input tables for the temperature sensors and fake the input so I can shut down the engines.

Then I'll have to change the password so no one else can access the system and reactivate the propulsion. After that, all I have to do is get out of there alive.

It's not easy, but it might work. Maybe. There are still a lot of details needing work. I need to communicate with the guys and make sure they're ready to come as soon as I stop the ship. I also need to disable the ship's communications so they can't ask for help, nor organize to resist. Finally, I must find some place to hide through it all, now that, for all intents and purposes, I'm on my own.

39

PETRA

obody was more surprised than Emma to find herself on a bus to Petra the next morning. Basuki had taken her clinics in exchange for her covering his in Egypt, since he wanted to see the pyramids. Linda and Dana made the same deal, so Basuki and Linda stayed on the *Sea Horse* while Emma and Dana took the special crew bus to Petra.

Sitting in the back by the window, she watches the rambunctious crew, most excited to have a day off. The men exchanged their drab uniforms for short shorts and T-shirts bursting with color, and they chat, laugh, and play like kids on vacation. Emma can't help but smile.

It's joyful, but hectic. She wouldn't mind it if the cacophony of hip-hop, Bollywood, and pop music coming at her from opposite directions would mellow a bit. But they're entitled to have some fun, she thinks, and turns to the window. The two-hour drive from Aqaba to Petra's visitor center in Wadi Musa is all uphill. As soon as they left the sea behind, the mountains, wild and barren, surrounded them. There's not much else: a village here and there, square blond houses ringed by tall walls looking deserted; a few lone trees with dusty leaves throwing meager shade; a scraggly lone bush. But not a flower, not even a blade of grass breaks the barren earth that the merciless sun baked into a crust.

The view opens once in a while, letting the eye run over strange rock formations clustered together like sheep, or glimpse at the hazy purple horizon miles away. The striking landscape is both majestic and forbidding, speaking of a hard life.

"I've never seen anything like this," Dana says.

"Neither have I. It's both beautiful and ruthless."

Something in her voice draws Dana's attention, and the nurse's warm eyes turn to her with worry.

"How are you holding on, Emma?"

"I do my best to hang in there. You?"

"Me too. The other night was terrible, even though Sue was such a miserable bitch. And that night was just one of many. Sometimes I get so tired of all this that I tell myself that I should pack and leave, but I have no better place to go. Working on ships was my ticket to a better life and the freedom to see the world. I would never have seen Petra if I'd stayed home, so it's worth it. For now. Is it worth it to you?"

"Probably not."

"Why don't you go home? Don't get me wrong, you're a good doctor, and I love working with you, but you don't look well. It's like you've shriveled since you came on the ship. I wonder if you take all this too personally, like it's your fault if people die."

"Well, it is."

"No, it's not. They are all adults who made their choices. No matter what killed them, it's not you. You tried to help them, but nobody can save them from themselves. Just like nobody can save us from ourselves but us."

Something in Dana's words sounds frighteningly true.

Nobody and nothing can save Emma from herself. Nothing can divest her from her memories, her insecurity, and her desperate loneliness. Not even leaving home to roam the world, or struggling to be the best doctor she can be. Whenever she saves a life, she thinks herself lucky. Every time she doesn't, she knows it was her fault.

The bus finally stops, and the scorching heat hits them like a blow as soon as they step out of the overworked AC. They take the uneven, dusty path along the *siq*, a deep narrow gorge cut through rock whose steep sides hide them from the sun. The trail is long and hot, but fascinating. Eager tourists rush down the trail toward the site, but the ones coming uphill seem to be in no hurry.

Along the trail, young men with sharp eyes drag long-eared donkeys and suspicious camels saddled with colorful blankets, trying to entice tourists for a ride. One approaches Emma to offer her a camel, but she laughs and shakes her head no.

"I wouldn't either," a voice behind her says. "The donkeys are so tiny it feels like I should carry them, not the other way round, and the camels are ill-tempered beasts. You never know when they'll spit and bite."

It's Archie, and Emma can't help but smile. He's grown on her since they first met, and his conversation is always stimulating.

"Do you happen to have firsthand knowledge of camel behavior?"

"You bet. I spent a whole year here, and everything we needed was brought in and out on camels, from tools and water to garbage and toilet paper. No wonder they're so grumpy."

A cart drawn by two galloping horses rushes past. They get way too close to Emma, and Archie pulls her out of harm's way. A second one follows, raising more dust. They go so fast the horse drivers' patterned headscarves flutter behind them as they stand to whip the horses, and Emma winces.

"They're just kids having fun," Archie says, but Emma shrugs.

"I don't think the horses would agree."

"Probably not. See their scarves?"

"Yes."

"Those are *keffiyehs*, and they're worn all around the Middle East. The nomadic Bedouins wore some made of cotton, silk, or wool, but the cheap ones you can buy today are polyester. They fold them diagonally and secure them with that coiled headrope, the *aqal*, to keep out the sand and the sun."

All of a sudden, the narrow siq opens to reveal an entire rock-carved city gilded by the morning sun, and the view takes Emma's breath away. A majestic rose-colored building stands across a wide plaza. It looks like a cathedral, but it's one with the rock. The tall, slender columns, their elaborate capitals reminding Emma of a Greek temple, are just bas-reliefs. So are the statues guarding the dark entry into the rock where the mysterious city lives.

"Petra is over 2500 years old and covers over 100 square miles. That building is the Al-Khazneh, the treasury, one of Petra's most elaborate tombs. It was built as a crypt in the 1st century AD during the reign of Aretas IV Philopatris, the Nabatean king. His daughter Phasaelis was Herod Antipas's first wife. Herod divorced her to marry the wife of his step-brother, Herodias, and speaking against this marriage was why John the Baptist lost his head."

"Why do they call it a treasury?"

"The legend says that the Egyptian Pharaoh and his men escaped the Red Sea, and he created the Khazneh by magic to safeguard his treasury while pursuing Moses. This whole place is imbued with legend, and it feels magic, even though a lot of the intricate details have eroded. See those sculptures? The four eagles are supposed to take away the dead people's souls, and the dancing Amazons with double axes protect the mausoleum. The twin statues that guard the entrance are Castor and Pollux, two Roman demigods who lived between the Olympus and the underworld."

"If Petra's founders were Arabs, why are there so many Roman and Greek elements in it?"

"The Roman Empire expanded eastward and took over Petra in A.D. 106. That's why the city preserves the Roman vibe. The Nabataeans were traders; Petra sat on the important incense trade route and became their capital. Since they were accustomed to the desert and skilled in harvesting rainwater, they built an entire system of cisterns, channels, and dams to store water, allowing them to thrive here. Petra is a UNESCO World Heritage Site and one of the New Seven Wonders of the World, alongside China's Great Wall, Rome's Colosseum, Mexico's Chichén Itzá, Peru's Machu Picchu, the Taj Mahal, and Rio de Janeiro's statue of Christ the Redeemer."

The long ride back gives Emma plenty of time to think about everything she saw and helps her put things into perspective. Compared to the birth and disappearance of this amazing civilization, her worries feel small. But then she gets back, and all hell breaks loose.

40

LEILA

L eila wakes up with the worst hangover of her life. Every move sloshes her brain inside her skull like an overfilled bucket, sending her thoughts into a spin. *What the heck did I drink?* she wonders, then remembers she didn't. She may have had the worst night of her life, but alcohol had nothing to do with it.

"Mommy?"

Ayisha sits at the window in her pajamas, hugging her pink dinosaur and sucking her finger. Her round dark eyes are worried.

"Yes, honey?"

"Are you sick? Should we go see the lady doctor that brought me ice cream so she can make you better?"

Sick? She is sick, but that kind of sickness no lady doctor can fix.

"I'm fine, honey. Are you hungry?"

Ayisha shakes her head no, but the clock above the TV says it's time for lunch, and she hasn't even had breakfast. The child needs a good, nutritious lunch, but Leila doesn't have the energy to fight with her.

"How about ice cream?"

A wide smile spreads across Ayisha's chubby face, and her missing front tooth is so endearing it makes Leila smile.

"Let's brush our teeth and go get some ice cream, OK?"

Ayisha nods and follows her to the bathroom. They brush their teeth and their hair and exchange their pajamas for T-shirts and shorts, then head upstairs to the buffet. The ship is eerily quiet. Something feels odd, but Leila can't put her finger on it. She glances outside. The ship is not moving, and Leila's heart skips a beat. Has Selim managed to strand the ship already? Are the terrorists on their way?

Cold sweat runs down her back, soaking her T-shirt. She wonders whether she should take Ayisha back to their cabin and lock the door, when she realizes they are docked along a pier. That is not what he planned. This must be a scheduled stop, but her brain got so muddled she forgot. She sighs with relief and follows Ayisha to the ice cream bar.

"What may I have, Mommy?"

"Whatever you want, my love."

The child looks at her with worried eyes. She's not used to such largesse, since she usually only gets dessert if she finishes her veggies, but Leila has no time to argue with her right now. She's too busy figuring out what to do.

She sips on an iced tea, watching Ayisha eat a monster ice cream topped with whipped cream, chocolate syrup, and sprinkles. A rivulet of melted ice cream drips down her chin onto her T-shirt, but Leila doesn't notice, as she thinks about last night's conversation.

Selim plans to disable the ship and deliver it to his buddies. He said it himself, but Leila has a hard time imagining it. She's known him for years, and he was always passionate about Palestine. She understood his devotion and even found it endearing, like seeing someone you love being obsessed with quilting, rock music, or cats.

But this plan of his is nothing like quilting or collecting cats. Somewhere along the way, he went off the rails, and he's about to cause a full-fledged catastrophe, whether to the ship and everybody on it or to himself. Either way, she must stop him. But how?

Talking to him will do no good. He won't listen to her. He's so blinded by his obsession that he can't see the enormity of what he's doing by condemning all these innocent people to a terrible fate. People will die, there's no doubt. Even if she and Ayisha managed to escape, innocent people would still lose their lives. And those who survive won't fare well. Leila has heard what happened to hostages before, and she dreads thinking about that. But Selim doesn't see or doesn't care. Either way, he won't listen to her.

She could try to warn someone on the ship, but who? The captain won't bother to see her, and the security people will think she's crazy. And she would have to confess to her part in the story and admit that she drugged the engineer, stole his stuff, and tried to break into their network. They'd put her in jail. Selim said that Ayisha would end up in foster care, and he was probably right. Still, that's better than dead. Or hostage to a band of terrorists.

But she can't bring herself to turn him in. Despite everything, she still loves him, and she knows he loves her, even though he forgot. There were so many small acts of kindness to her and Ayisha: He stayed up when she had a fever, he never forgot her birthday, and brought her breakfast in bed on Mother's Day — they have to mean something. He loves her, and he's the only one to love her child. She can't repay his love with betrayal. He would hate her forever, and he'd never return to her.

But, more than anything, she must keep Ayisha safe. She should have disembarked this morning and taken her home.

One way or another, she would have found a way to make it back. But she'd been so exhausted she slept until noon.

But... maybe it's not too late. The ship is still here. They can leave now, and she'll figure out how to get home later.

Her heart fills with hope. That's it. That's what she needs to do. She won't betray Selim, but she'll get Ayisha out of here, somewhere safe. Too bad about the ship and the hostages and all, but they are not her responsibility. Ayisha is.

The girl finishes her ice cream and licks her spoon with total focus.

"Let's go, baby."

"Go where?"

"Go home."

"Home? Is Daddy coming?"

"He will, later. Let's go."

Back in her cabin, Leila gathers the essentials in her backpack: a change of clothes for Ayisha, toothbrushes, her inhaler, a few toys. She grabs her computer bag and slides in her laptop, her iPad, and her phone. She checks she has her credit card and money. All there.

Still, something's missing.

She looks around the room, in the closet, in the bathroom.

What is it?

When she finally realizes, her stomach turns, and she rushes to the bathroom to retch.

Their passports are missing. Selim must have taken them last night.

They can't go anywhere. They are stuck on this doomed ship.

41

READY

I smile at the grumpy security guard who checks my ID
as I return to the ship, telling myself that tonight's the
night. I won't have to put up with this crap anymore.
I'm torn between relief and worry, but I'm as ready as I can
be, and I can no longer wait.

This morning, I went into Aqaba and talked to the guys. I
could have done it from here, I guess, but it felt safer to get
off the ship. It took me forever to get them, and, truth be
told, they weren't that excited. It's too far, they said. It would
be much better if I could wait until the ship got further
south, closer to the Bab El Mandeb Straight. But I said no.

That would mean at least two more days and one more
night, because tomorrow we're supposed to stop at Safaga,
the entry port for Egypt, and they plan to overnight there to
allow for shore excursions to Cairo and the pyramids. But I
can't wait two more days. Between four dead bodies and a
crazy woman who might blow up on me at any moment, I
am running out of time.

It will take them longer to make it to the *Sea Horse*, but

once I've done my part and disabled it, there isn't that much of a hurry. The ship won't go anywhere without its engines.

They finally conceded, and we agreed on the time and the place so I can complete my plan. Sadly, I had to give up on sabotaging the communications. The radio room is on the ninth deck, near the navigation room, while the ECR, the engine control room, is down below, in the ship's bowels. There's no way I can do it all alone, so I had to pick my fights. My first priority is the engine, and communications are a distant second. That might mean that subduing the ship's security when the boys arrive may get tricky, but they should manage. There's only so much one man can do.

The ECR is on the second deck, next to the machinery room, which is good, because nobody on the upper decks will hear the noise coming from down there until it's too late.

I start getting ready. I had planned to use sleeping gas rather than nerve gas at first, for two reasons. First, because unlike hostages, dead people are worth nothing. Second, because it's less risky for me. Should something go wrong with the mask, I'd rather fall asleep than drop dead. But then I changed my mind. I don't know how long it will take me to get everything done, and the last thing I need is to have those folks waking up while I'm still struggling.

That's why I'll take the nerve gas grenades. I also need my laptop and the cables. The gas mask, of course, which is awfully cumbersome and impossible to hide. The oxygen tank.

I pocket my stun gun, just in case, and the engineer's key to the room. I hope they didn't discover that it was missing and disable it. If they did, it's over.

That's it. Time to go big or go home. Only there's no going home. I am committed, and there's no return.

I take a shower to wash off the sour stress sweat and lie

down for a nap, but sleep won't come near me. I turn on the TV to watch the news from Gaza, hoping that gets me pumped up, and it does. After five minutes of watching children bleeding, black-clad women wailing over dead babies, and crying men struggling to pull out their loved ones from under rubble with their bare hands, I feel like I've drunk rocket fuel. I can't fail this mission. I'd rather die. I am so wired I can hardly wait until midnight, when I need to go.

I remember Leila, and my mouth fills with bile, so much so that I have to spit it out. That spoiled bitch betrayed me. She said she loved me and would do anything for me, and then...I can't think about her anymore, or I'll get sick to my stomach. So, to get myself together, I pray.

I make sure I face Mecca and thank Allah for trusting me with this mission. I bare my soul and tell him how proud I am to do his work, and how joyous I feel to give my life for this mission to succeed.

God's grace pours into my soul, filling my heart with joy, and I thank him again for his mercy. Then I lie on my bed and fall asleep.

The alarm wakes me up two hours later. I put on my Kevlar vest, then my oxygen tank, and I hang my loaded backpack in front.

I pull the black burka from the bottom of my suitcase and put it on. The shapeless black garment covers me from head to toe, with only a slit for my eyes. I glance in the mirror. I look like a fat, pregnant, hunch-backed Muslim woman. Not even my mother could recognize me like this.

I thank Allah once more and head to the door.

42

THE MISSION

The hallways are empty and quiet as I head down the stairs, glad the plush carpets soften the sound of my footsteps. I stop in front of the medical office door I know so well. I listen for a minute, but no noise comes from inside, so I get in through that door and then slide out the other, as usual. I walk down the third deck, then take the stairs to the second, quiet as a cat. But the stress takes its toll. My hands are clammy, and I can feel every heartbeat in my temples.

I pass one door, then another, before getting to the one labeled Engine Room. I pass that one too, and head to the next one, labeled Restricted Area. Do Not Enter.

This is it.

I open my burqa, take off the hood, and pull out my gas mask. I call it a gas mask, but it's a whole SCBA, a self-contained breathing apparatus with an oxygen tank.

I place the mask on my face and tighten the straps, making sure I have a perfect seal, then grab one of the gas grenades from the backpack on my chest. It doesn't look like much. It's just a white plastic canister no bigger than an orange, but it's a Russian S-28, gas-filled, striker-release hand grenade customized for this operation. It uses the K-510 fuse, similar to the other grenade fuses, but this one is shorter and has an internal thread. The S-28 burns for 10 seconds and produces a thick lethal smoke.

I trust my soul to Allah and remove the safety pin. I hold the grenade in my left hand as I wave the engineer's key in front of the lock.

Nothing.

I whisper something, not sure if it's a curse or a prayer, and try again, but still nothing. They must have disabled it.

My heart sinks and my hands shake as I grab the doctor's key from my pocket and wave it in front of the lock as a last resort.

The lock clicks, and the door opens. The walls are covered in screens, panels, and equipment, telling me this is indeed the ECR, as I had hoped. It's just as I remembered from the simulation. With one exception.

Four men stare at me from the long counter on the left. They're so shocked their eyes pop out of their sockets, and their jaws hang to their knees. No wonder. Between the gas mask and the burqa, I must be quite a sight.

The blond in the white shirt must be the officer. He's the first one to recover and reach for the alarm, just as I throw the grenade. Time stops as the plastic canister bangs against the wall, then drops to the metal floor with a clang and rolls to his feet. He freezes in mid-squat as the thing touches his well-shined shoe, hisses, and bursts into flames, letting out a thick cloud of gas. It's Sarin, NATO designation GB, and it's colorless, odorless, and lethal, even at low concentrations. Unless an antidote is administered immediately, death occurs within seconds to minutes after inhalation, through suffocation from respiratory paralysis. And no one around here seems ready to administer an antidote.

The smoke fills the room. The men choke and scream, trying to reach the door, but the sound of the machinery next door drowns their pleas for help, and the door is too far. They turn blue as they writhe on the floor, clutching their throats and scratching out their eyes. I don't need to worry about them anymore, so I get to work.

The long wall to my right is covered with panels, high power warnings, gauges, and alarms monitoring every detail of the ship's functioning. The benign door flanked by fire extinguishers behind it warns Do Not Enter Without Head-phones, and must lead to the machine room. There's a coffee station in the far corner, and a shelf with flotation devices for emergencies, and all sorts of crap, but none of that is what I need. What I need is the engineer's control table, which in my simulations was just a simple desk with a monitor and a place to plug in my laptop.

The big red button protected in a clear plastic case, the emergency stop push-button for the main engine, calls me. Oh, how I wish it was that easy. But stopping the main engine would leave the others working, and unless I disable the whole system, they'll restart it faster than you can say sabotage.

Straight ahead, a large monitor shows me the deck cameras. That ought to be interesting later, but for now, I need to do what I came here for.

I find a port and plug in my laptop. The system asks for my credentials, so I pray to Allah once more and type them in. I hope the system recognizes the computer, since it's been hooked into it before.

But it takes its sweet time. I sweat like a pig under my mask and my burqa, and I crave a sip of water or at least a breath of fresh air, but there's none of that here. Not for me.

The login screen disappears. Thanks to the all-merciful Allah, I'm in.

43

THE DEEP SLEEP

er wet red hair plastered to her head, Sue smiles, offering Emma John the Baptist's severed head on a platter.

"What do you want me to do with him? He doesn't even have a chest to do CPR," Emma says, and Sue throws the platter at her. The head rolls, and the platter clangs as it hits the floor. Emma wakes up.

Her nightmare is over, but the noise is not. Her pager and her phone are both ringing. Emma picks them up and silences them as she glances at the clock above the TV. Twelve minutes to one, its green face says, and Emma grabs her sneakers, snags her doctor's bag, and blasts through the door wondering what's going on. The only good news is that there's no Bright Star signal, so maybe nobody has died. Yet.

Out in Medical, Dana is getting the Bright Star bag. Linda is on the phone. Her eyes meet Emma's and she raises her hand, telling her to wait.

"Just a second, sweetheart," she says into the phone. "Stay right there and don't hang up, OK? I'll just tell the lady doctor what you told me."

She covers the mouthpiece and says, "It's the little girl who was here for her asthma last week. She says her mom won't wake up."

A cold shiver runs down Emma's spine.

"What's her cabin number again? Never mind," she says, and runs after Dana, who takes the stairs two at a time. Five floors later, they're both panting and sweating as they knock at the door, but no one answers.

"Let's just go in," Dana says.

Emma looks for her masterkey but can't find it. *I lost it somewhere,* she thinks, and curses between her teeth as Dana opens the door with hers.

The only light in the room comes from a bedside lamp. Ayisha, wearing the same pink pajamas, sits on the loveseat by the window, hugging her dinosaur. Her mom lies curled on her side in the large king bed and doesn't move when Dana turns on the light.

Emma smiles at the child but rushes to check on the woman. Her face is pale and her eyes closed, and she doesn't seem to be breathing. Emma touches her neck. It's still warm, and, thank God, there's a pulse. She pulls off the covers and watches the chest rise and fall with every slow breath. Too slow, Emma thinks, counting to eight breaths in one minute.

She rolls her on her back and checks her pupils. Pinpoint. She rubs her knuckles into her sternum, hard. The woman moans and tries to push her away, and Emma sighs with relief.

"Looks like an opiate overdose."

"You want Narcan?"

"I'll take the spray. And let's check a glucose, just in case, but we need to take her downstairs anyhow. Can you send the stretcher team? And take the kid with you. She doesn't need to see this. Find someone who can look after her. I'll wait here."

Dana checks a glucose while Emma sprays a dose of naloxone in the woman's nostrils.

"Glucose is 102." Dana grabs Ayisha's hand to take her downstairs, but Ayisha shakes her off.

"I stay with Mom."

Emma kneels by the child's side and puts her hand on her shoulder.

"Listen, Ayisha, I need your help. I need you to go to the medical office and tell the nurse lady exactly what happened when you tried to wake Mom up, so we can figure out what's wrong and how to help her. I will stay with her and we'll bring her down soon, OK?"

Ayisha still looks uncertain, until Emma says, "And the nice nurse lady will get you an ice cream."

Ayisha nods and takes Dana's hand, but Dana stares at Emma in consternation.

"Where do you think I'll find ice cream at 1 a.m.?"

"Room service," Emma says, and they're off.

Emma turns to the patient. Her vitals seem OK. Her lungs and heart sound fine, her abdomen is soft and benign, and the legs have no edema. Nothing appears abnormal besides the slow breathing rate and the pinpoint pupils. She examines her arms for needle tracks, but finds nothing. Odd, she thinks, and checks around her nose, looking for traces of snorted white powder, but there's nothing.

Something feels odd about this woman, Emma thinks, and looks around the room, trying to make some sense of her. She's sounded peculiar since the first time they met. She said she was going from London to Dubai to meet her husband via a cruise starting in Istanbul. The second time, when Emma came to check on Ayisha, the woman couldn't wait to see her gone. She pretty much told her not to come back, and that was weird too.

But, just like the woman, the cabin keeps its secrets to

itself. There's nothing remarkable other than a bunch of scattered clothes and toys. And even that is weird, since the last time Emma was here the cabin was immaculate.

Someone knocks at the door. The stretcher team has come to take the woman down to medical. She's still asleep as they arrive to find Ayisha eating ice cream in the waiting room. Emma ruffles her curly hair as she passes by, taking the woman to the ICU.

"Let's do the usual — monitor, IV access, labs, drug screen. And let's give her just aliquots of IV Narcan. Just 0.04 mg every minute until her heart rate gets to 10, but no more. The last thing we need to do is to throw her in florid withdrawal."

"You think she's a habitual user?"

"I don't know, but I don't want to find out."

They're still working on the sleeping woman when the alarms go off. All of a sudden, the ship starts rocking and bouncing like a cork on the waves.

44

MISSION ACCOMPLISHED

I did it.

My hands shake and my eyes burn as I watch the engines shut down and the ship's speed fall to zero. Thank Allah, they responded to the overheating signal I faked to override the real input. All I have left to do is change the password to ensure they can't get in and undo all my hard work, and then get out of here. Alive, preferably.

I push the Change Password button.

"Are you sure you want to change the password?" the system asks.

"I've never been surer," I mumble, and the system concedes.

I need a password simple enough to remember but complicated enough so that nobody else can figure it out. Ayisha@March4*2019. I type, and the system asks me to repeat it. I do. I can't imagine anyone else knows Ayisha's birthday, so this should be safe.

Now that I'm done, I'd better get out of here while I can. Lights flash and alarms wail all around me. The ship gets thrashed about on the waves, now that it no longer has any speed, and I know they'll be coming any moment. They might not dare come in here if they see my gas mask and the bodies on the floor, but I have less than an hour's worth of oxygen left. I need to get out before my tank is empty.

I crack open the door. Nobody in the hallway, so I blast out toward the stairs just as the door to the engine room opens and two mechanics come out.

"Go back. Go back now," I shout, aiming my Glock toward them. Between my mask and their headphones, they can't possibly hear me, but they get the message when they see my finger on the trigger. They run back in and slam the door. Smart guys. I run to the stairs when I notice an elevator to my left. Boy, that's tempting. But it's too risky, I think, and keep on going.

I'm halfway up to the next deck when two security guards block my way, their guns drawn.

"Drop the gun and put your hands up in the air," one of them shouts, sounding like he means business.

I panic for a moment, but then I remember they're so incompetent they probably don't even know how to use those guns, and I pull the trigger. I don't really want to kill them, but I'm past being nice and they stand between me and my way out.

The first one screams and grabs his shoulder. The one behind him crashes down the stairs and takes the first one with him. They'd take me too if I didn't flatten myself to the handrail to make room.

I'm not curious enough to wait and see what happens, so I run up the steps as fast as I can, then turn left to get out. Ten feet away, two officers in white shirts block my way, ready to stop me. *Sorry, boys. Can't do that.* The first bullet hits the tall one in the temple, and a fountain of blood erupts from his left eye as he crumbles. The second one glances at him and steps aside to let me pass. *Now that's smart,* I think, and rush forward. I'm about to leave the crew quarters for the passenger side. *Once there, I should be safe,* I think. With my universal key, there are a million cabins I can hide in, and I'll take some hostages to keep me safe while I wait for my friends to arrive.

I'm just six feet from the exit when the door cracks open. I don't know who's behind it, but they must have had time to regroup, and I only have a few bullets left in my gun.

I draw a deep breath and change plans. It's two in the morning, so Medical should be empty. I'll block the doors and wait for the guys to take the ship. Nobody will be stupid enough to break in there when they know I'm armed to the teeth.

I wave my key at the lock and it clicks. I barge in and slam the door behind me. Thank Allah, I'm safe. I turn around.

Ayisha, her eyes as big as saucers, stares at me.

45

AN ARMED MAN

In the ICU, Emma rechecks the woman's vitals when she hears the door slam outside. She goes to see what's going on and freezes. Six feet away, a person in a gas mask and a burqa stands by the door with a gun. They aim the gun at her and signal her to back off.

I never thought I'd end up like this, Emma thinks. She steps sideways instead of back, to cover Ayisha, and studies the person. He's not very tall, but by the wide shoulders, shoes, and big hands, he must be a man. And whatever he came here for, he doesn't have good intentions. But what shocks Emma most is that she's not afraid. Numb, maybe, but not afraid.

"Stop this nonsense. You're scaring the child. What do you want?" she asks.

He stares at her for a moment, probably wondering whether to shoot her, then points at the ICU door.

Emma takes Ayisha's hand, takes her to the ICU and sits her in a chair by the bed where her mom is still asleep. She looks around for something she could use to protect them, but there isn't much. The shelves are loaded with ET tubes, plastic urinals, ventilators, and dozens of medications, but nothing that looks remotely like a weapon, unless she counts her stethoscope. Or the trocars for the chest tubes, which are known to kill people, but can't compare to a gun. Even the canes and the crutches are in the X-ray room down the hall, not here.

"Who is that?" Ayisha asks.

"I don't know," Emma says.

"What does he want?"

"I don't know that either."

"I want my daddy," the child says, and Emma's heart aches for her. What a terrible day she's having. First, her mom wouldn't wake up, then this.

Emma caresses her hair and asks, "Ayisha, tell me something. Why did you try to wake your mom in the middle of the night?"

"I had a bad dream."

"What did you dream of?"

"I dreamed that Mommy and Daddy had a fight, then Daddy did something to Mommy and she fell asleep. I tried to wake her, but I couldn't."

Emma nods, listening to what's going on outside. She hears him go from door to door, opening them and closing them again. *He's making sure there's nobody else here,* she thinks, and she's glad she sent the others to deal with the emergency call from the bridge. But if they come back…

He opens the door to her office and spends a lot of time there before coming back out to check the X-ray room and the two quarantine cabins along the narrow hallway, and Emma has a thought. If he steps out the back door into the staff quarters, she might have time to run out the door with Ayisha. But her mom is still here. She can't run and leave her behind. Still, she needs to save the child. But how?

"Ayisha?"

"Yes."

"If that man outside goes into another room, I will open the door for you to run out, OK?"

"Why?"

"I need you to go find the nurse lady and tell her what happened. Tell her that a strange man came into Medical, and he sent us into a room. I'll stay here and take care of your mom while you go find the nurse, OK?"

"OK."

"As soon as I open the door, you run up the stairs, then turn on the corridor as fast as you can."

"Why?"

"So you can find her sooner."

"Will she give me ice cream?"

"You bet."

Children! With the ship going up, down, and sideways, Emma's stomach is twisted in knots. She can't even think of food, but the kid wants ice cream. Good for her.

She hears the door to their little kitchen open and close, then the door to the staff quarters opens, and Emma's blood whooshes in her ears as she waits. Forever, it feels like. When the door finally slams shut, she doesn't know which side of the door he's on. She counts to ten, then drags Ayisha to the passenger's door and shoves her out.

"Run!"

She closes the door and heads back into the ICU. Time to wake up the sleeping beauty. If she had to choose between being in acute withdrawal and being unconscious in a hostage situation, she'd take the withdrawal. She picks up the Narcan syringe and pushes the plunger all in, then grabs a scalpel from the box and drops it in the cargo pocket of her pants. Her hands shake as she draws a massive dose of succinylcholine into a syringe and puts it in her other cargo pocket. She's not keen on the sux, which is a muscle paralyzer; she'd rather have ketamine, but that's locked in the controlled substance cabinet in her office, and she can't get to it without a nurse. But the sux, which is lethal, is not a problem. That would be sad if it weren't hilarious. Or is it the other way round? She doesn't get to make up her mind because the door opens again. He is back.

46

ONLY ONE BULLET

Not a second too soon, she drops the empty vial in the sharps container by the bed as she hears his rushed steps. A second later, he's at the door. His gas mask hangs around his neck now, revealing a shiny beet-red face, and Emma recognizes Sexy Man, even though he doesn't look particularly sexy at the moment.

"Where's the kid?" he asks.

"She left."

"Where?"

Emma shrugs. Her scalp prickles as he lifts the gun to her left eye and tightens his finger on the trigger. He looks like he knows exactly what he's doing, and that's good. A quick, clean death is something Emma always hoped for, after seeing so many ugly deaths on the job, even from firearms. You'd think you can't miss when you shoot yourself in the head, but you can. And it's horrific.

A hundred thoughts race through her head as she watches his index finger squeeze the trigger. She recalls the teenage kid who shot himself in the mouth three years ago. He'd been outed as gay and couldn't stand the bullying, so he stole his father's gun to kill himself. He wanted to make sure he couldn't miss, but he did. He blew up his lower face, but the bullet crossed his neck without touching his brain, so he lived to see himself in a mirror. And it wasn't pretty.

But this guy seems to know what he's doing, and Emma is ready. Taylor is a grown-up, and she has Victor and Margret to help her bring up little Hope. Hanna will make sure Guinness gets back home to Margret. The dog will probably miss her, but she'll be much loved and well cared for. And that's everyone she's responsible for. The others can take care of themselves.

She looks into the black hole of the gun, seeing the trigger move ever so slightly, when a blood-curdling scream makes her jump. The man startles too, and takes his eyes away from her, but Emma is too shocked to take advantage. She turns to see that Ayisha's mom woke up, and she stares at them like she saw a ghost. No wonder. With his burka sweeping the floor and the gas mask hanging from his neck, Sexy Man is a sight to behold.

"What the heck are you doing here?" he asks, turning his gun toward the woman.

Now if we were in the movies, I'd jump him and grab his gun, Emma thinks. But this is not a movie, and she's not a sexy blonde, fast as a snake and strong as a bear. More like the other way round, she thinks, and bursts into laughter.

Both the man and the woman turn to stare at her. Emma shrugs.

"Sorry. Don't mind me. But it's a good question. What are you doing here?" she asks the man, but the woman speaks first.

"You miserable, filthy creep! You stole my passport, so I couldn't take Ayisha out of this shithole. And drugged me, so I couldn't turn you in."

"Me? I am the creep? After you swore you loved me and

you'd do anything for me? It was the two of us against the whole world, remember? And now it's you and the whole world against me."

"You idiot! You lost your mind! I thought you were a decent man with an endearing passion, only to find out you are a psychopath. You'd do anything and destroy anyone for your obsession. I hate you! I hate you like I've never hated anyone. You lied to me, you used me, and you put my child in danger for your stupid pipe dream that will never happen."

"Sure it will. Just wait. My partners should be..." He glances at his watch. "Only half an hour away."

"And then what?"

"They'll take the ship, and I will have fulfilled my mission."

Emma glances from one to the other, struggling to make sense of this, but she fails. The only thing that's clear is that the ship is in danger, and so is everyone on it.

What can she do?

Now that she knows this, she's no longer expendable. Five thousand lives are in danger, and Emma is the only person who knows it, other than the conspirators. She'd better stay alive to warn the others.

She glances at the door, wondering if she could dash out without being shot, now that they are busy with each other. But the man with the gun stands between her and the door, and there's no way she can squeeze out unnoticed.

"Your mission, you fool? You call taking five thousand innocent hostages a mission? None of these people did anything to hurt your beloved Palestine. They are innocent! And if you think the world will be eager to help them after what you are doing, think again. You and the other lunatics like you give Palestinians a bad name, making them all look like abductors, terrorists, and murderers. You're sabotaging the mission you say you want to accomplish, and bringing shame to your country."

The man's face twists with fury. In one smooth move, he lifts the arm with the gun and shoots the woman right between her eyebrows. Emma was right. He is a good shot.

The woman writhes like she's seizing, then settles. Her wide-open eyes watch something she'll never see as the monitor's beep goes crazy, then flatlines.

Emma steps toward the bed, and the man lifts his gun.

"Stand back! Stand back now."

Emma ignores him. She checks the woman's pulse, then closes her eyes with gentle fingers. Nothing else she can do. Thank God she sent away the little girl. She's already seen more than enough.

47

HOSTAGE

He didn't shoot her. He pushed her to the waiting room at the end of his gun, told her to sit, and zip-tied her legs to one of the waiting room chairs. He then took off his burka, his oxygen tank, and his mask, set his backpack on the nurses' desk, and turned to her. His cold eyes measured her from head to toe and seemed to find her lacking.

"Do they like you up there?"

"I beg your pardon?"

"Up there? The captain and the officers, do they give a shit about you, or are you just a thorn in their side?"

Emma stops to consider.

"Mainly a thorn in their side. Not all of them, but the captain would probably rather have me dead."

His eyes widen in surprise.

"Really? What did you do to him?"

"I've been a thorn in his side."

He nods like this makes perfect sense.

"I'm not surprised. Still..."

The old phone on the desk rings, and he freezes. He

glares at it like it's a venomous snake and makes no move to pick it up. Emma crosses her arms on her chest and watches.

Five rings later, the phone stops, then starts again.

"You may want to pick that up if you're planning to negotiate," Emma says.

"What makes you think that I am?"

"I don't imagine you came here to admire my outstanding looks. But since you're here anyhow, you may as well find out what they're worth."

He gives her a side glance and picks up the phone.

"Hello?"

Emma can't hear the other side of the conversation, but she sees his eyes slide from her to the ICU, where the dead woman lies, and back. He shrugs.

"Yep. I've got your doctor. Would you like her back?"

Emma forces herself to stop listening, since she knows she won't like what she hears. Captain Van Huis wouldn't want her back if she came free. Less so if he had to pay some unthinkable price for her. She's on her own.

She glances back at her doctor's bag sitting on the counter in the ICU. *It may as well be on the other side of the moon,* she thinks, glad she at least has a scalpel, when his voice breaks into her thoughts.

"She's alive, alright."

"OK."

He brings the phone over and hands Emma the handset.

"Hello."

"Emma?"

"Yes?"

Who the heck is this? Emma wonders, before realizing it's the captain. He has never called her Emma before.

"Are you OK?"

"Yes."

"Anyone else there?"

"No one alive."

"Stay strong. We'll try to negotiate your release."

"You may have bigger things to worry about," Emma says, and the captain goes silent.

"Is something about to happen?"

"Soon."

"That's enough," the man says and grabs the phone from her hand. "You want her back?"

He waits for the answer, then nods.

"Good. I want a helicopter to take me to Sana'a. Once we get there, I'll let her go."

He listens, then shakes his head.

"I don't care how hard it is. Get moving. If you want to see her alive, make it happen. The sooner the better." He hangs up and turns to Emma, his eyes hard.

"I hope he likes you better than you thought."

48

A LONG WAIT

This wait is driving me crazy. I pace until I can pace no more, then I sit at the desk in the medical office and look around to distract myself, but there's not much to see. This is a terrible place, and it smells awful, like iodine, blood, and sickness. I wish I was outside, but it can't be long now.

I glance at my watch. It's almost three. They should be here any minute. I wonder what I should do. The smartest thing would be to stay locked here until they take the ship, but where's the fun in that? I'd much rather partake of the action, but I'm not sure how to go about it. The last thing I need is to do something stupid. I should be patient and stay put. That way, I'll be ready to take advantage of any opportunity.

I check my watch again. Nothing changed. This wait is killing me. I stand to pace again, then I remember the office has a porthole. I stick my nose to it and look outside, but there's nothing. Just the sea, dark and forbidding, throwing us around. I go back and pace some more.

The computer. I wonder if it's connected to the deck

cameras. I turn it on, but it takes forever to warm up. Where the heck did they get this dinosaur?

It asks for a password. Fortunately, the user ID and the password are written on the mouse pad, so I can log in. Their security is a joke, but the darn thing is slower than a dead man's eye, as Grandma used to say. Every screen takes forever to load. By the time I finally get to the cameras, ten more minutes have passed, and still nothing. Nothing on the camera either. If I didn't know better, I'd think the entire ship was asleep.

I glance at the doctor. Her eyes closed, she leans back with her head against the wall. I'll be damned if she's not asleep. That takes some nerve. Not a shrinking violet, this one. She's surely not my type, but she did me a favor when she let Ayisha go. I'm not the kid's father, but still. I don't want her here, especially not when I had to shoot the bitch. I'm glad she wasn't here to see it, though a child hostage would bear more weight. And it would keep the doctor busy, rather than give her time to come up with who knows what shenanigans. Fortunately, she doesn't seem in any hurry to escape.

I check my watch. 3:13. They are late.

Of course they're late. They had hundreds of miles to travel in the dark to find us. We're no more than a needle in the haystack here, in the middle of the sea. They'll be here.

I stand to pace again. The woman doesn't even bother to open her eyes. I go to the little kitchenette to grab some water, then rush back, worried she'll try something, but no.

The phone rings. There's no good reason to take it, but I can't stop myself. Patience has never been my strong suit, and this wait is driving me crazy. I need to do something or I'll self-combust.

"Hello."

"Hello. I might have gotten your helicopter."

"You might have? You did, or you did not?"

"Still working on it. How's the doctor?"

"Asleep," I say, and glance at her, but her eyes are open. She's watching me.

"Can you put her through?"

"And wake her up? Sure."

I hand her the phone.

"Yes. No."

I grab back the phone.

"Tell me about that chopper."

This is bullshit, of course. I want no helicopter, because I'm not going anywhere. But that gives them something to think about. Better that they plan how to ambush me as I board the helicopter than wonder what's going on and get ready for my friends' arrival.

"It's a medical helicopter coming from Jordan. They might get here at noon, if the weather doesn't interfere."

"Noon? Are you nuts? That's hours away. Listen, my friend, I don't think we are communicating. I hate to do that, but unless you cooperate, I'll send you the doctor in pieces. Starting with the fingers, then going up. I suggest you put a rush on it."

I slam down the phone and look at the doctor. She's back to looking asleep, but I know she can't be. She's playing possum.

I glance at my watch. Almost three thirty, and still nothing. And, deep inside, I start to worry.

I go to the bathroom and splash some water on my face. My eyes burn like I haven't slept in weeks. Some coffee would be good. I go to the little kitchenette and start a pot of coffee.

A funny little noise comes from the waiting room. I drop the pot and rush back. The doctor is working on her ties.

She's already cut one of them with a scalpel, and she's working on the second.

I slap her, hard. She crashes to the floor with the chair, and the scalpel flies to the other end of the room. I point the gun at her face.

"Don't do that again. Ever. Stand up."

She grabs the chair and struggles to her feet.

"Sit."

She does.

"Put your hands back."

I bind her wrists together, then tie her ankles to the chair again. There's an ugly red mark where I slapped her, but otherwise she looks fine. I'd better be careful.

It's four o'clock and still nothing, and I'm getting worried. Whatever the reason, they are an hour late and I'm losing it.

49

THE FIGHT

Emma straightens her achy back in the hard chair that has made her bottom numb and watches the man pace around the room like a caged tiger. Her cheek still burns from his slap, and she's so mad at herself she could puke.

She watched him get more and more antsy as half an hour turned into an hour, then two. She did all she could to look compliant, but when he finally went to the kitchen to make coffee, she knew it was time. She managed to saw through the first zip tie, even though thin-bladed scalpels aren't made to cut hard plastic. Still, she was half done with the second, and she'd have been free in ten more seconds if she hadn't kicked the chair and made noise.

She's lucky he didn't shoot her because she knows darn well that he's not planning to go anywhere, so he doesn't really need a hostage. All he needs is to wait for his buddies right here, so she's no more useful to him than the dead woman next door.

But why did he talk to the captain?

Just a red herring meant to put them on the wrong path.

Having them plan how to catch him when he leaves, instead of worrying about a more immediate threat. But thank God, the captain understood.

"Emma, should we expect an external attack?" he had asked.

"Yes," she said.

"Not from inside?"

"No."

The man took the phone before she could add anything, but the captain got the idea. Now that she has warned them as best she could, all she needs to do is to stay alive.

He wouldn't have any qualms about shooting her. She saw him kill the mother of his child without blinking, and he hasn't even glanced at the body since then. Emma watched him, wondering if he regretted shooting her, but if he did, he gave no sign.

He goes into her office, looks outside through the window, then returns to pace again, walking with the unintentional grace of a lethal large cat. *If he had a tail, it would twitch,* she thinks.

He must have killed the mechanics, and Sue. But why? He probably wanted them quiet. But about what?

All of a sudden, the silence explodes in an ear-piercing cacophony. The alarms wail. A gunshot rings, then another, and another. The man runs to the office to look outside, then back to the computer to check the deck cameras. There's a weird disconnect between the raging firefight outside and the monitor's soothing sonata.

The speakers spring to life.

"This is your captain speaking. All crew, present immediately to your designated stations for plan T. Repeat. Plan T. All passengers, do not leave your cabins. Repeat, passengers, do not leave your cabins. We are addressing an external threat, and your life can be endangered in any of the ship's public areas. Do not, I repeat, do not come out for any reason. Crew, present to your designated station for plan T."

It's finally happening, and Emma feels a strange wave of relief. She doesn't need to worry about it anymore; she just needs to deal with it.

She glances at the man. Leaning against the desk with his head cocked to the side to hear better, he listens to the message and his face glows with awe.

The speakers go quiet, but the firefight intensifies. *Whatever's going on up there, it can't be easy for the crew,* Emma thinks, wishing she knew more about the ship's emergency plans.

The man is flushed and breathing hard, and he looks like he can't take it anymore. It's easy to see that he'd rather be up there, but that would mean giving up his safe spot, and he hesitates to do that when he doesn't know what's going on up above.

He cracks open the door to the crew quarters and peeks out, then lets it slam shut. He goes to the passengers' door and does the same, then sits on the chair to watch the deck cameras.

"I need to use the bathroom," Emma says.

He stares at her like she said she needs to win the Preakness, but that's not her problem. She really needs to pee.

He shrugs. "This is a bad time."

"It may be a bad time, but this is when I need to go."

He sighs and cuts the ties off her legs.

"Go then. But don't be long."

Emma turns around to present her tied wrists.

"What?"

"Can you pee like that?"

He hesitates, but she's interfering with his watching the cameras, so he cuts her free and nods toward the bathroom.

Emma sighs with relief and sits on the toilet. She rubs her

wrists and her ankles to get the blood flowing, then looks around for anything useful. But there's nothing but the urine specimen cups and toilet paper. Not even a plunger. She sighs, washes her hands, and rinses her face in cold water, then unlocks the door.

She still has her sux in her pocket. That would take a few minutes to work, but if she can inject him and stay alive for five minutes, she's golden. But how the heck can she do that?

She opens the door to find herself facing his gun.

"Take everything out of your pockets and drop it on the floor."

50

A HARROWING MARCH

Trussed in her seat like a chicken, Emma feels like the stupidest person who ever lived. He took her sux, and with it, her last hope to get away. She should have known better, though she's not sure what she could have done differently. But it's too late to worry about the past. What can she do now? Nothing comes to mind, other than cursing up a storm.

She bites her lips to stop her tears when the ship suddenly goes quiet. The firefight stopped just as suddenly as it started; the battle upstairs must have come to an end. The ominous silence is even more disturbing, since she can't tell who won and who lost. Have the terrorists been defeated, or did they take over the ship? Emma doesn't know, and apparently the man doesn't either, since he watches the cameras with an obsessive focus, looking for an answer.

His face twisted with rage, his fists tight, he stands to pace again. All of a sudden, he stops and opens the backpack he'd dropped on the desk when he tied her to the chair. It feels like a year, but it was only a few hours ago, and Emma can't help but wonder at the strangeness of time.

He pulls out stuff and sets it carefully on the desk, one by one. There's a cheesy plastic grenade looking like it came from Walmart, and two smaller green ones. There's also a stunner, a magazine for his gun, and a strange curved knife with an ornate handle. He pushes aside the gas mask and the oxygen tank.

He checks everything, then picks the gun, the stunner, and the knife and puts them in his pockets. He cocks his head to listen again, but the ship is as silent as a tomb. He turns to Emma, his cheeks flushed and his face twisted with rage.

"Are you ready?"

"For what?"

"For your last hurrah."

He cuts the tie holding her wrists together with the evil-looking knife and hands her the white grenade.

"Are you familiar with Sarin?"

Emma's heart freezes. She learned about it in medical school, but hoped to never ever need that knowledge. Sarin is a nerve agent, potent enough to kill a man in seconds by paralyzing his respiratory muscles.

"I am."

"Good, because that's what you're holding. Don't drop it," he says, and pulls the pin out of the grenade before cutting her ankle ties.

"Let's go, doctor. Let's find out what the world holds for us."

With his gun in his right hand, he opens the door to the passenger stairs to let her pass, and Emma walks out in a daze. The cheesy white thing she holds in her hand can kill them and everyone else around them. And there are five thousand people on this ship.

"Head up," he says.

She takes the stairs, praying they don't meet anyone. Her

mouth is dry, and her feet feel heavier than lead as she crawls up the steps, holding on to the grenade with trembling hands. Fortunately, there's not a soul anywhere.

One floor up is the promenade deck, where she walked with Guinness so many times. Thinking of the dog brings tears to her eyes, and she bites her lips to stop them.

"Get out on the deck. I want to see what's going on."

That's tricky, since the doors are awfully heavy, and she's terrified she'll drop the grenade. But she manages to push the door open with her shoulder and squeeze out. He follows right behind her, his gun bruising her ribs.

A brisk wind smelling like the sea blows in her face, cooling her burning cheeks. She hears the waves, but it's too dark to see the sea down below.

"Turn left," he says.

She turns left, glad there's nobody there. The ship rocks and twists between the waves under her feet, and the wind's direction changes. Instead of the sea's salty scent, it brings the acrid smell of gunpowder and the stench of blood and bowel contents. Emma's skin prickles into goosebumps.

"Keep going," he says.

Holding on for dear life to the gas nerve grenade, Emma struggles to put one foot ahead of the other. She holds the plastic canister so tight her fingers go numb. She knows it's all over if she lets go of the lever, but her years of managing epistaxis in anticoagulated patients taught her to switch hands without ever letting go. She switches the grenade from one hand to the other. With the gun in her back, she walks all the way to the bow, but there's nothing else to see other than complete emptiness. At the bow, she turns left and heads back toward the stern. That side is just as empty. She wonders if this is good news or bad when the gun bruises her spine again.

"Go back in and head upstairs."

For a moment, she thinks about throwing the grenade into the sea and taking her chances with the gun. But her chances with the gun are precisely zero. And she's curious to find out who won.

She finds an entry door and complies.

51

FACING DEATH

Holding the grenade in both hands, Emma struggles back in through the door. Her heart beats to break out of her chest as she crawls up the stairs waiting for someone to attack. She's moving so slowly she's surprised that he doesn't berate her to go faster, but he must be as anxious as she is.

It takes them forever to climb the five floors to the upper deck. Nothing moves other than their own steps and their shadows. The *Sea Horse* is so silent it feels dead.

They reach the navigation deck at the stern, inside the Ocean Bar. Emma knows it well, but now it feels like she's never seen it. The place was hopping every time she was here: women with makeup thicker than facemasks showing off their finest; flushed men chasing free drinks; loud music; and migraine-inducing blinking lights. Now it's dark, quiet, and so dead it may just as well be a morgue.

"Head toward the bow."

Emma turns left and pushes the door. The stench of gunpowder and death hits her like a punch, and she freezes into place.

So this is where they fought.

The sun deck with its lovely blue pool looks devastated by a tornado. Pool chairs are piled helter-skelter against the walls. Towels and chairs are scattered everywhere. Pools of dried blood turn into bloody foot tracks converging toward the bridge. But despite all the blood, there are no bodies on the ground, and Emma wonders what they did with the wounded and who's looking after them.

"Go straight."

He burrows the gun's barrel into her side, and Emma steps forward, avoiding the pool of blood. Her heart's racing and her hands shake as she skirts the swimming pool to approach the metal stairs leading to the deck above, the one with the radars. Straight ahead, the bridge is so dark and quiet you'd think they're all dead. The sharp wind cuts through her scrubs like she's naked, chilling her to the bone, and her frozen fingers are numb. She clutches the grenade to her chest, afraid she'll drop it.

"Stop."

Other than the howling of the wind rattling some loose metal parts, the silence is eerie. That must mean that the terrorists lost. Otherwise, they'd be out here, celebrating, Emma thinks. That can't be good news for him.

He must know it, too.

"Turn around. Go back the way we came."

"Stop right there," a voice speaks from the darkness. "Drop the gun."

Emma's heart quickens as he grabs her by the neck and pushes the gun's barrel against her right temple. Hard.

Oh, how she'd love to elbow him in the plexus and shove him away, like Antonio taught her. But she holds a lethal grenade and has a gun to her head. A wrong move and she'd be dead in a hurry.

"Don't move, or I'll shoot her. And she won't die alone."

"Is that so?"

"She holds a grenade full of Sarin. If she drops it, you're dead."

"No, we're not. We're far enough, and we are behind doors. But you will be."

The gun trembles against Emma's temple, crushing the skin. *The bad news is that I'll have a black eye tomorrow,* she thinks. *The good news is that I'll be too dead to care.*

"What do you want?" the voice asks.

"My helicopter."

"Your helicopter came and left, after dropping a few of your friends. You should have been here sooner."

The arm around Emma's throat tightens, and she wonders what sort of game the captain is playing. He's acting like he wants to enrage this lunatic. But why?

"I'm here now. Does your offer still stand?"

"What offer?"

"A helicopter to Sana'a, and I let your doctor live."

"I don't know. Things got complicated when your friends dropped by. I'm not sure that deal still stands. I'll have to consult with the…"

"I don't care who you consult with. You get me that helicopter, or I'll make sure you're all dead," he says, pushing Emma forward toward the bridge.

She has trouble keeping her footing on the slippery deck and tightens her hold on the grenade as he forces her forward.

"Open the door."

He lets go of her neck and shoves her forward so hard she loses her balance and drops to her knees. She holds on to the grenade for dear life, wondering why he let her go, when a sharp cry of rage and pain gives her goosebumps. A curse follows, then a low deep growl, and Emma turns around.

A dark shadow hangs from the man's shoulder, growling

and trying to rip him to shreds. Emma would love to help, but there's something else she has to do. She struggles to her feet, runs to the railing, and lobs the grenade into the sea as far as she can.

A gunshot rings. Guinness cries.

The dog pulls the man to the ground and lets go of the shoulder and latches onto the throat. The gun clangs to the deck as the man puts his hands around her throat and chokes her. The dog doesn't seem to notice as she growls and rips into his throat like a fury.

"Drop it, Guinness. Drop it."

Guinness lets go and comes to lick Emma, but she's shivering, and her tail is down. She is hurt.

"It's OK, baby. It's OK. I'll take good care of you." Emma hugs her as the bridge door opens and people come out of the shadow.

"Call a Bright Star," Emma says. "We have two wounded to care for."

52

TREATING GUINNESS

Ten minutes later, Emma is down in her office, examining Guinness, while Basuki looks after the terrorist in the ICU.

"Are you sure?" Dana asks. "Shouldn't we do it the other way round?"

Emma's anger bubbles to the surface.

"Why? Because she's a dog, she deserves less care than a freaking terrorist?"

Dana's eyes widened.

"Of course not. But they say we're not supposed to treat our own family members."

Emma shrugs. She'd be glad to trust Guinness to a vet, but there's none on the ship. She's the closest they have.

"Can you get an IV?"

"I guess so. Where?"

"The front legs. Shave her if you need to."

Guinness gets her legs shaved, possibly the first German shepherd with that sexy feature, while Emma looks for the bullet. But it's not easy. The dog is covered in blood, some of it hers, and it's hard to find a wound under all that fur.

Emma palpates every inch of her, looking for signs of pain, until she finds an induration. It's the bullet.

"It's in her back leg, but it tunneled under the skin before getting there from her left shoulder. It touched no vital organs, but it must hurt like hell."

"What do you need?"

"Let's do some ketamine. She's about 70 pounds, and at 1.5 mg/kg, let's give her 50. And we'll also give her a dose of antibiotic and half a liter of fluid."

"How do you know the ketamine dosage for dogs?"

"I don't. But dogs are people too. If that's not enough, we'll give her more."

Precisely one and a half minutes after getting her ketamine, Guinness's eyes close as she catches a nap. Emma makes a small incision with the scalpel and uses a forceps to pull out the bullet without trouble. She does her best to wash the wounds with saline, then closes them with two staples.

The patient is still asleep when the procedure is done. She looks fine to Emma, but Dana has trouble obtaining her vitals.

"Even the child cuff is too big for her. I can't get a blood pressure."

"I think she'll be fine. Give her a little water when she wakes up, and call me if there's any problem."

The bond between Guinness and Emma is so strong that Emma doesn't need to see any vitals to know she's OK, like she didn't need them to know when she wasn't. She pets her soft head once more and goes to the ICU, where Basuki is working on the man.

"How are you doing?"

Basuki's eyes light up.

"Terribly. He's not in good shape."

"No wonder. What's the problem?"

"I think he suffered a spinal injury. Or a stroke. He doesn't seem to be able to move his left side."

"Anything else?"

"Not that I know of."

"Let's get him stabilized and fly him to some place that can look after him. There's nothing more we can do about that here."

Basuki grabs his phone.

53

GOODBYES

It's Emma's last evening on the *Sea Horse*, and it looks like every single person on the ship came to her clinic.

"What on earth got into them? Why is everyone here this evening?" Emma asks when Linda comes into her office bringing another stack of charts.

The nurse laughs.

"They're here to see you, dear."

"Me? What for?"

"Are you kidding? The brave doctor who saved the ship from a fate worse than death? Have you seen the news lately?"

"I did not. I stopped watching the news long ago. And I didn't save the ship from anything. The crew did. I barely kept myself alive."

"Why don't you tell them and see if they believe you? You know, Emma, people love unlikely heroes. And don't get me wrong, you're a great doctor and such, but you're not the kind of person people think about when it comes to thwarting a terrorist attack."

"She's like Superman. She looks ordinary until disaster strikes," Dana says, bringing another chart.

Linda laughs.

"I like that. Doctor Superwoman."

"Oh, stop it, both of you. Are we done yet?"

"Not yet. But you'll like this one."

One of the pretty receptionists walks in holding a child by the hand, and Emma's heart sinks when she recognizes Ayisha. She thinks about her every day, and she wanted to see her, but she worried that seeing her would remind her of the night her mom died and upset the child even more. She stayed away, but felt guilty.

That night when Emma sent Ayisha out of Medical, she promised to take care of her mom. And what a lousy job she did! First, she watched the woman get killed, then she helped capture her dad. Ayisha may not know all of that, but Emma does. She finds it hard to believe the child would want to see her.

But there she is. With her riot of black curls and her sad eyes so big they take half her face, she looks even smaller than she did.

"Hello, Ayisha. How are you doing?"

"OK."

"Are you sick?"

The child turns to the receptionist, who shakes her head.

"No, Ayisha. You are not sick. Tell the nice lady doctor why you came."

The child hesitates, then says, "I came to say goodbye. And to thank you."

Thank me? What for? Emma wonders. More importantly, what will happen to her? Her mother died, and if he pulls through, her father will likely spend his life in jail. Who will look after Ayisha?

"Where are you going, Ayisha?"

The child looks at the receptionist.

"You will disembark tomorrow in Dubai, then go home to Grandma and Grandpa."

Emma would like to hug her, but she's not sure the child wants to be touched, so she just smiles and nods.

"I hope you have a good trip home, Ayisha."

The receptionist takes her hand to leave, but Ayisha shakes her off. She runs to hug Emma.

"Thank you for the ice cream," she says, and Emma bites her lip to stop her tears.

As soon as Linda locks the doors after the last patient, Dana pulls out a bunch of flowers from under the desk and they hand Emma a parcel wrapped in silver paper.

"Something to remember us by," Linda says, and Emma's eyes fill with tears.

"I need nothing to remember you by. Are you kidding? How could I ever forget?"

"Well, I meant remember us fondly."

Emma opens the box. The gift is a wood-carved *Sea Horse* replica, just half a foot long, but it has such intricate detail that Emma can even see the porthole of her cabin.

"This is magnificent! It's a work of art."

"It's made by an Indonesian artisan. He used to work on the ship, but now that he's retired, he makes a few of these each year for very special people."

"I can't thank you enough. For this, and for everything you've done for me on the ship."

"You deserved it. We'll miss you, Emma."

"I'll miss you too."

But she won't miss the ship. She won't miss living tethered to the phone and the pager without a moment to herself. She won't miss the passengers' entitlement and the drills and the cultural sensitivity classes and getting lectured by the captain for every minor transgression. *I won't miss any of that,* she thinks, as she gets ready for her last dinner.

54

LAST SUPPER

Emma is late, as usual. By the time she gets to the Ambrosia, Hanna, Nok, and Archie are flushed and so animated that it's easy to guess they're past their first drink.

Their cheer grows when they see her. Archie stands to pull her chair before the maitre d' can grab it. They hand her a glass of wine and lift theirs in a toast.

"To my dear friend, who's like family to me. I'll miss you, Emma," Hanna says.

"To my very special friend. Emma, you may not know it, but you're the only woman who can make my husband even angrier than I can," Nok says.

"To the very unique lady that made this trip unforgettable," Archie says.

"You guys make me blush." Emma tastes the wine and sighs with delight.

"I thought you'd like it," Archie said. "You have fine taste in wine."

"In people too; otherwise, she wouldn't be our friend," Nok says, and they all laugh.

"What are you most looking forward to when you get home?" Hanna asks.

Emma doesn't need to stop and think.

"Taking Guinness for a hike in the woods. I won't even take my phone. Just the two of us and the mountains."

"I can see how much you missed your freedom. I just wish they had mountains in London," Archie says.

"Why don't you come visit?" Emma asks, then wishes she hadn't. But it's too late.

"I'd love to. Maybe I will. When would be a good time?"

"The fall is beautiful. Other than November, when it rains a lot, the leaves are gone, and the trails are muddy and slippery. But winter is beautiful, with thick snow covering the trees and brilliant blue skies. Do you snowshoe?"

"Never did."

"Well, it's a good time to start, then. I'm going to miss you all," Hanna says, her lovely face sad.

"Why don't you come too?" Emma says. "You don't have to hike. The drives through the Adirondacks are beautiful. You can spend lovely mornings reading by the window and the evenings sitting by the fire with Guinness."

"I just might. How does Christmas sound? I don't love Christmas on the ship. There's just too much damn cheer for my taste."

Emma laughs.

"Well, you won't have to worry about that at my place. Last year, we decorated a tree in the yard. As in, Taylor hung some lights, and then Guinness pulled them down."

"I just might. How about you, Nok?"

Nok wrinkled her pretty nose and pretended to shiver.

"Are you kidding? I don't do snow. It doesn't work with high-heeled sandals, and the cold ruins my complexion. But I'd love to have you all in Thailand. There's no snow, but I know I'll find plenty to keep you entertained."

"What will you do when you go back, Emma?"

"I don't know yet. I'll try to get myself together for a few weeks, then look for a job."

"At sea?"

"Oh, no. Never again. It takes a certain kind of person to do that, and that's not me. I don't know how others do it, but I can't."

"So you'll find a job in the ER?"

"Probably. I might go locums."

"What's that?"

"You work in various places across the country. They pay for your hours, your flights, and your hotel, as long as you commit to a number of shifts. You get to see a lot of places. Not only in the states; I have colleagues who worked in the Virgin Islands and Guam. Others settled in Australia and New Zealand. I bet I'll find something."

"What will Guinness do when you travel?"

"Stay with my daughter, I guess, but you have a point. Maybe I'll stay put for a while."

When the maitre d' comes to take their order, Emma smiles and asks for her last cioppino.

"You're tempting fate," Hanna says.

Sure enough, she has barely started eating when her pager goes off.

55

THE DEPARTURE

E mma looks around her cabin for the last time. Hard to believe she can regret leaving this terrible place, but she can't escape a stab of nostalgia. This is where Fajar told her about his incredible relationship with his wives. This is where she listened to Dr. Majok's desperate plea for help. This is where she spent so many dreadful nights getting paged to deal with the terrible things that kept happening on the *Sea Horse*. But, since life's sense of humor is dark, this is also the only place on the ship she found peace. And this is where she went dry.

It took her a long time, but one evening, the worry of being unable to deal with the endless disasters became worse than the pain of her memories. Her crazy mother. Her cheating husband. The loss of her son. Taylor.

That's when she quit drinking and let herself suffer. She allowed herself to feel the hurtful feelings she didn't want to deal with. Remember the harrowing memories she wanted to forget. She had to, because lives were at stake. She could get drunk to forget her pain and let people die, or she could suffer, but be available when she was needed. The choice was easy, but keeping it was hard enough.

But now it's finally over. She pulls the bottle of Johnny Walker from the bottom of her closet and opens it. The smell of whiskey fills her nostrils, making her mouth water. Now that she's free, she can get as drunk as she wants. Nobody will die because of that.

She studies the amber-colored liquid that's calling her like an old lover, remembering how good it feels to be numb. She sighs, empties it in the toilet, and heads out.

She waves at the crew members aligned in the hallways, then gets to the exit where the security guard checks her ID and salutes.

"Have a good trip, Doctor."

"Thank you."

Antonio, as handsome as always in his tired T-shirt and shorts, waits by the door. He takes her in his arms and gives her a bear hug.

"Good luck, Emma. It was a privilege knowing you. Knock them dead out there, will you?"

Tears fill Emma's eyes. She owes Antonio a huge debt of gratitude for teaching her to channel the anger of her ugly past into her fighting, and thus help her unburden her heart. She doesn't know how she will keep up her training without him, but she'll find a way.

She takes the gangplank to the pier.

Straight as a poplar in his pressed white shirt, his shoulders heavy with gold, Captain Van Huis is waiting. *He wants to make sure I'm gone,* Emma thinks.

"Good morning, Doctor."

"Morning, Captain."

"I wanted to wish you a safe trip home."

"Thank you."

"And thank you for everything you did for the *Sea Horse.*

It was quite an experience having you with us. You certainly kept things interesting."

There may be a hint of a smile on his narrow face as he hands Emma a package.

"This is for you."

What on earth can it be? Emma wonders. She's so curious she can't wait, so she opens it in the taxi taking Guinness and her to the airport.

It's an engraved wooden plaque. "To Dr. Emma Steele, forever grateful. The Sea Horse and all its men."

Emma's eyes fill with tears once more, but Guinness licks them off.

EPILOGUE
ONE YEAR LATER

The mean, icy rain turned to slush, then to snow, as is fitting for a Christmas Eve. The snow covering the pine trees is so heavy the lower branches touch the ground, and Guinness loves it. She thought they were sticks, so she tried again and again to take them with her until she figured out that they belonged with the tree. Then she decided to take the whole tree, snow included, but the tree disagreed. They were still fighting when Emma dragged her back inside and did her best to wipe her with a towel before letting her loose in the kitchen.

Emma checks on the turkey. It's plump and golden, and it looks done. Smells done, too. The aromas of pepper, cumin, and garlic fill the kitchen and make her mouth water. She sets the pan on the counter to let the bird rest while she plops a can of cranberry sauce into a bowl and prepares to make gravy. She didn't prepare appetizers — not only do they ruin your appetite, but they make you fat. But she likes to do turkey, stuffing, and gravy, and even sweet potatoes once in a while. For dessert, she bought Ben and Jerry's ice cream. It won't be half as spectacular as Amber's Christmas dinner tomorrow, but she stopped competing with Amber long ago. If anything, she feels grateful to her for taking Victor off her hands. It sure didn't feel like that eleven years ago, but that was then, and this is now.

Merry noises of chatter and laughter come from next door, where Taylor and the kids have been decorating the tree under Guinness's close supervision. Truth be told, the tree looks crooked, and the top is almost bald, but it's wonderful to see Taylor behave like the adult in the room. She still has her moments, of course — she always will. But she's a wonderful mother to little Hope, who turned into a strong-willed toddler, and Emma can't help but smile, remembering what Taylor said when they arrived.

"I don't know how you did it, Mom. I really don't. Every single day I want to pull out my hair and hide in a dark room to cry. But then I think of you and soldier on. When does it get better?"

Emma chuckled.

"When you get to be a grandmother," she said.

Taylor shuddered. Emma laughed and hugged her, surprised at how easy it felt to be with her daughter. But she wasn't kidding. Dealing with Hope will only get harder before it gets easier, but there's no point in telling that to Taylor now. She'll find out by herself.

The doorbell rings just as Emma roasts the flour — her secret to a smooth gravy. She first roasts the flour, then adds the drippings, not the other way round. But this is too important a moment to answer the door.

"Can you get the door, please?" she shouts at Taylor.

She drips the turkey juices into the gravy pan, stirring all along, and watches the gravy thicken. Looking good. She sets it to the side of the range to keep it warm and turns to check the sweet potatoes when someone hugs her from behind.

Emma resists throwing an elbow to the solar plexus, like

Antonio taught her. It's been more than a year, but she still jumps whenever someone touches her unexpectedly. *I guess I'll never grow out of that,* she tells herself, turning around to see Frank.

"I got you this," he says, handing her a massive bunch of yellow mums shaped like giant spiders, with their long, twisted petals. *At least they're not venomous,* Emma thinks, inhaling the flowers and hugging him back.

It's strange how comfortable she feels in his arms. Last year, when she returned from her adventures on the *Sea Horse,* she couldn't stand seeing people for weeks. When Christmas came, Archie declined, which was good. But then Hanna emailed her.

"Is it alright if I bring a friend?"

What could Emma say but yes? As long as Hanna was happy...

It turned out that the friend she brought was mutual. It was Frank, the quirky biologist passionate about all things venomous Emma had met on her first cruise. He had liked her a lot. She had liked him too, but not enough. Still, one year later, she rediscovered how much fun he could be, quirks and all. She's still not ready for a serious commitment, but she's ready to have a little fun. They started a long-distance relationship and see each other a few times a year, but live alone. For now.

"Dinner is ready. Everybody, wash your hands and come to the table," Emma says. She sticks the yellow mums in a deep green vase and sets them in the middle of the table Taylor set. She did a great job, Emma tells herself, admiring Vera's delicate china, the silver cutlery, and the sparkling crystal glasses. Vera would be proud.

Little Hope runs in, all smiles and looking adorable in her Christmasy green velvet dress. She hugs Frank's knees and asks him to lift her up and twirl her. Taylor follows. Her eyes are tired, but she's as beautiful as ever, and she's all grown up now. Margret comes next, her lovely warm face lit by a smile. They stand by the table and wait.

Finally, a little girl with a riot of dark curls rushes in, wiping her hands on her frilly pink dress.

She shows her hands, still wet, to Emma.

"Is this good, Mom?"

Emma ruffles her hair.

"It's perfect, Ayisha."

* * *

GUINNESS FANS, check out **Becoming K-9**, her memoir, where she'll tell you what she thinks about humans.

To learn more about the ER, read **Stay Away From My ER.**

AFTERWORD

Dear reader,

Thank you for reading *Take Lives*. If you enjoyed it, **please leave a review** to help other readers like yourself.

Guinness fans: check out **BECOMING K-9**, A Bomb Dog's Tale. It's her heartwarming memoir that will pull at your heartstrings. It's also the book I'm most proud of.

ABOUT THE AUTHOR

Rada was born in Transylvania, ten miles from Dracula's Castle. Growing up between communists and vampires taught her that humans are fickle, but you can always rely on dogs and books. That's why she read every book she could get, including the phone book (too many characters, not enough plot), and adopted every stray she found, from dogs to frogs.

After joining her American husband, she spent years studying medicine and working in the ER and on cruise ships all over the world, but she still speaks like Dracula's cousin.

And, while the characters and situations in *Take Lives* are fictional, the ports of call, the medical cases, and the snippets from the crews' lives are based on Rada's personal experience.

facebook.com/RadaJonesMD
bookbub.com/profile/rada-jones
instagram.com/radajonesmd

MORE BOOKS BY RADA JONES

K-9 HEROES Series: Six bomb dogs telling their own stories.

"Until you, hoomans, learn to sniff each other's butts so you can read each other's thoughts, you'll need us, dogs, to guide you, love you, and make you better people."

Corporal K-9 Guinness Van Jones.

"I laughed, I cried, I laughed more, I sobbed. I was skeptical when I started the book but could not put it down."

Amazon review.

K-9 HEROES series

STAY AWAY FROM MY ER: Wobbling between humor and heartbreak. A collection of ER essays.

Not for the faint of heart... You'll laugh, cry, and marvel at the alien world that is the ER.

"As an old OR nurse, I recognized many patients. The disappointing thing about this book was its BREVITY. I laughed until I cried at some of her stories."

Amazon Reviews

STAY AWAY FROM MY ER

FUN TRAVELS IN THE GOLDEN YEARS: Cheeky travel memoirs to Italy and Kenya.

Two intrepid curmudgeons. An SUV with red plates. Ten thousand miles of twisty roads. What could go wrong?

"It was entertaining to learn how Rada and her husband lived and learned during their travels through Italy. Rada's book was not just entertaining, but also very informative. I'm now better equipped to deal with unexpected Italian experiences. You will love this book!"

Amazon Review

FUN TRAVELS IN THE GOLDEN YEARS series

SOON TO BE X: A contemporary novel about Thailand, heartbreak, and new beginnings. To be released in spring 2025.

SOON TO BE X

THE SAGA OF THE DRACULA BROTHERS: A based-on-true-facts series of historical novels about Vlad The Impaler published as RR Jones.

1442. In Wallachia, the line between loyalty and betrayal is thinner than a sword's sharp blade. Den Of Spies is the gripping true story of Vlad Dracula, the child who would become Vlad the Impaler.

Warning: This series includes dark, gritty scenes of sexual assault and violence.

The SAGA OF THE DRACULA BROTHERS series

EXCERPT FROM BECOMING K-9

Who knew training humans was so hard? You'd wonder why. They aren't that stupid. It takes them a while, but they eventually learn when you want out, you're hungry or you're thirsty. They can even talk to each other by making noise with their tongue. How weird is that? Even my brother Blue, who's the slowest of us all, knows that the tongue is for lapping water and panting to cool down.

Mom cocked her head and licked my nose.

"That's the best they can do, dear. They have no tails, their ears don't move, and most don't even have enough fur to raise their hackles. No wonder they're confused and need us to guide them. And that's what we do; that's our life's work. But we need to choose them carefully."

Mom was on her sixth litter and very wise. Beautiful, too, with her long muzzle, amber eyes, and smooth, shiny fur, all black but for her golden legs and loving pink tongue.

She glanced at Yellow, who chased his tail instead of paying attention, and growled. He hung his head and sat in line with the rest of us to listen.

It was a lovely summer day as Mom homeschooled us in Jones's front yard. The warm wind tickled my nose. I bit it, but I caught nothing. I tried again, but Mother threw me a side glance, so I closed my mouth and sat still.

"Boys and girls, today's the day. People will come to check you out and choose which one to take home. They don't know it, but it doesn't work that way. You choose your humans, but choose them wisely. Sniff them all, then pick the ones that smell like food if you want a good life. You may sometimes get bacon, maybe even grapes. Humans say dogs don't eat grapes, but that's poppycock. They just want to keep them for themselves. My grandma was a pure-bred Alsatian, and she loved Riesling. I never had Riesling, but Concord isn't bad."

A shiny strip of drool dripped from Mom's mouth. She licked it off and inspected us. We were seven: three boys and four girls. But that doesn't much matter when you're just ten weeks old. The only difference is how you pee. The boys don't know how to squat so they need something to lift their leg to, like a bush or a mailbox. How stupid!

"Why don't you just lift your leg, if that's what you need to do? What does the bush have to do with anything?"

Mom bristled.

"Leave them alone, Red."

I tried, but it was hard. I was the runt of the litter, so I had to prove myself all the time. Mom said I had a Napoleonic complex.

"What's that?"

"It's when you're the smallest, so you have to be meaner to show them that size doesn't matter."

I told you Mom is brilliant. She came all the way from Germany when she was just a pup. Our human, Jones, has two passions: German shepherds and history. Mom was his first German shepherd, and he spent lots of time teaching her things most dogs never heard about.

He still does, even now that she's old. He sits in his recliner and reads to her as she lays by the fireplace. Sometimes I listen in. There was a story about a dude named Hitler. Not a nice guy, but for loving German shepherds. Another one about that short guy Napoleon who tried to conquer the world while wearing funny hats. And one about some place called Afghanistan.

"That's a bad war, Maddie," Jones said, scratching the four white hairs in his beard. "Those Taliban, they are not nice people."

He calls her Maddie, but her real name is Madeline Rose Kahn Van Jones. He is Jones. The Van is for Van Gogh, some orange dude who got so mad he bit off his own ear. The rest is just for show, since people pay more for dogs with long names; they call that a pedigree. Mom's pedigree is longer than her tail.

As always, Mom was right. People came to see us, and they brought their spouses, their kids, and even their dogs to check us out and choose which one to get. Like, really? Jones said that only one out of twenty German shepherd owners is smarter than his dog. I don't believe it. I bet he fudged the numbers to feel better. You think you own a dog? Who feeds who? Who cleans after who? Who does the work, everything but making decisions? You, human, in case you didn't know it. You don't buy a dog; you hire supervision. But I digress.

My littermates and I wore colored collars so humans could tell us apart. There was no need, really, since we were all different, but humans couldn't see it. What color did I wear? Red, of course. I was small, but I was the queen of the litter, whether the others liked it or not.

A fat man in a Hawaiian shirt stopped to stare at me. He called his female.

"Look at this red one! Isn't he cute?"

She hobbled closer, leaning on her crooked stick. I love sticks, so I tried to take it. She didn't want to let go, but I insisted. They laughed.

"Let's get him."

Jones cleared his throat.

"Red is lovely, indeed, but she's a very active little person who needs a lot of attention. How much time do you plan to work with her every day?"

"Work with her?"

"Yes. Walk her, train her, and play with her."

They stared at him like he'd lost his marbles. He smiled.

"May I recommend Brown here? He's lovely, easygoing, and eager to please. He'll be happy to lay on the sofa watching TV. Or Miss Green? She's a polite little lady who gets along with everyone and never disappoints."

Brown left. So did Green, Yellow, and even White, while I stayed, waiting for my forever home.

"Take it easy, Red dear," Mother said when there were only two of us left—Black and me. "You need to soften up a bit; otherwise, you'll be left without a family. People look for easygoing dogs to fit into their lives, not for somebody to take charge. Though maybe they should, really, but they aren't smart enough to know that."

Her German accent made her words feel harsh. Have you ever listened to Germans? It's like they're constipated while they also have a cold. They keep clearing their throats, so their words come out like bullets from a machine gun. I don't speak German, but I love watching old war movies with Jones.

"What do you mean, Mom? What should I do?"

"Lick their hands, sweetheart. Wrap yourself around their feet and stare at them like they hung the moon."

"Are you serious?"

"Of course."

"But they're stupid!"

"Come on, Red, don't be so judgmental. You're just a pup, and you have so much to learn. A nice family will give you a good life. They'll love you, play with you, and spoil you. Knowing you have a good, safe home will lift a weight off my soul."

You think I listened? You've got to be kidding.

That's how I ended up in the military.

* * *

Read BECOMING K-9

Made in the USA
Columbia, SC
04 January 2025

51218282R00150